PRINTHOUSE BOOKS
PRESENTS

I0614827

Pulsations of A Heartbeat

Unholy Matrimony

Fiction

ANTWAN 'ANT' BANK$

VIP INK Publishing Group; Inc.
Atlanta, GA.

Unholy Matrimony

© 2015 Antwan 'Ant' Banks

PrintHouse Books

PrintHouseBooks.com

VIP INK Publishing Group, Incorporated

Printed in the USA

Cover art designed by SK7.

Editor: Shelby Oates

Published: 11-26-2015

Isbn – 978-0-9965-701-1-4

Library of Congress Cataloging-in- Publication Data

#2015953398

Antwan 'Ant' Bank$

1.Drama 2.Suspense 3.Urban Lit 4.Romance

They say that success isn't worth anything if you don't have someone to share it with. Rich finds himself in the exact situation with a flourishing detail shop and auspicious real estate investments. To make it all whole he decides to share everything with his lady, Melissa.

Melissa, a very successful financial advisor, is no slouch as she too has plenty to bring to the table. But, what Rich doesn't know about the love of his life is that he isn't her one and only. Every pulsation of his heartbeat bleeds for her love.

It's just too bad that the same can't be said for her.

Dedicated to my angel whose wings have yet to lead her my way; I have so much love waiting for you.

ANTWAN 'ANT' BANK$

Pulsations of a Heartbeat

Unholy Matrimony

VIP INK Publishing Group, Inc.
Atlanta, GA.

Table of Contents

Wedding Bells

An array of formally dressed men and woman fill the Westin ball room. Past the white cloth draped tables which held crystal glasses, porcelain white plates and stainless steel silver wear sit Rich and Melissa in the front of the room at a long satin laced table. On either side of them sit the bride's maids and groomsmen as the best man Kevin stands to make a toast.

"It seems like only yesterday that me and Rich flipped his first house. Now a little over a year later, I'm here making a toast at his wedding." Kevin raises his glass.

"This is to Melissa and Kevin: I wish you guys all the best, you two are made for each other."

Rich looks over at Kevin with a puzzled expression on his face and thought it was strange that his friend had so little to say.

"Baby what's wrong, why are you looking at Kev like that?"

"Oh, it's nothing Melissa!" Muah! He leans in and gives her a kiss.

"I love you baby, come on let's dance, everyone is waiting!"

How Deep is Your Love plays over the speakers as the guests follow the newly-weds to the dance floor. Lissa spots a strange woman approaching their best man as she and Rich make their way to the center.

"Rich! Rich!"

"What is it baby?"

"Who is that with Kev?"

"Oh that's Sybil, I think."

"Sybil! Who is that? Where's Brittany?"

"Shit, I don't know!"

Not amused by Kev and Brittany's drama, Rich calmly caresses Melissa's soft red cheeks, looks deeply into her pretty brown eyes, grabs two hand fulls of her nice round ass and began to sing the emotional penetrating words from Keith Sweat's love ballad.

"Why are you embarrassing me like this Rich? Stop grabbing my ass."

"It's all mines now baby, I done put a ring on it."

"Ha-ha! That's a start!"

Ring-Ring! Ring-Ring! Rich can see his new bride's gown light up just above her breast where she placed her phone every time it rings. Ring-Ring!

"Now why in the hell do you have that phone woman, can you at least turn it off!? This is our wedding day!"

"I'm sorry, hun, but you know I can't afford to miss any calls. A lot of people trust me with their finances! I have to stay readily available."

Ring-Ring! As her cell continues to ring, the wedding party began to look on with disbelief.

"Damn, just answer it already Melissa, come on let's go."

Frustrated Rich grabs her by the arm and walks off the dance floor then takes his seat behind the table as she walks in the opposite direction.

Ring-Ring! Ring-Ring! Melissa hastily makes her way out into the empty hallway.

"Hello!"

"Well, did you do it?"

"Yes Bill, I did it."

"That's not what we discussed Melissa, you shouldn't have."

"Listen mister, you have no room to tell me what to do! Besides your white ass is married already, so zip it!"

"I already told you that I was leaving her!"

"Yeah, you have been singing that same old song for 2 years now."

"But!"

"Don't but me! I have to get back to my wedding before Rich gets suspicious!"

"Well, we'll finish this conversation at the office Monday!"

"No we won't; I'll be in Dubai with my husband."

"Dubai!"

"Bye William!"

Bill didn't know what he was feeling as he paced back and forth from his office door then back to the cherry oak finished desk. Forty-five stories above interstate 75/85 he watched the mid-town traffic down below from his corner office window. Buzz-Buzz! Buzz-Buzz!

"Yes Nancy, what is it?"

"Mrs. Kennedy is on line one, sir."

"Ok you can put her through."

Mr. Kennedy sits on the corner edge of his huge executive desk then presses the speaker button on his office phone.

"Hello!"

"Hi Bill, the kids wanted to know if you were going to meet us at the Hawks game tonight?"

"Sure, I just need to wrap a few things up and I'll be right over."

"Ok darling, do you know what time?"

"I'm sure I will be there before the 1st quarter ends."

"Awesome, we'll see you in the suite, love you!"

"Love you too, honey."

William still didn't understand what he was feeling. He could still smell Melissa's Dolce & Gabbana perfume on the lapel of his Armani blazer. It had been 4 weeks since that intimate evening in Chicago and he refused to put that blazer in the cleaners, in fact it still rested on the coat hanger behind his office door.

"So who was that on the phone?"

"Oh, that was my boss. He just wanted to say congratulations."

"Damn, that guy can't live without you, huh baby?"

"Rich if you only knew."

"Come here and sit on my lap, we're about to cut this cake, Mrs. Blackmon."

"You couldn't wait to say that, I bet?"

"I think Melissa Blackmon has a nice ring to it, don't you?"

Muah- She leans down and kisses Rich on the lips to avoid answering the question. Deep inside she wonders if this was truly the right decision or was she just eager to be married.

"Ok Sir, let's cut this cake so we can get home, I am so tired; this has been a long day."

"Baby we still need to open all of those gifts over there and why are you in such a hurry woman?"

"I just want to get naked and lay in the bed with you hun."

"Well in that case, we can take the damn gifts home and open them there!"

"Oh you down to go now, huh? Just like a nigga. Ha-ha."

"Yep, they'll understand if we need to go handle some grown folks' business."

"Um hmm, I bet."

The excited couple walks slowly over towards the cake as they whisper softly amongst each other. Both of them knew that their family, friends and loved ones would be pissed once they told them that they were leaving. So Rich and Melissa entertained their guests just a few hours longer.

———————————

"Girl, this is a nice ass shop!"

"Thanks, Blu!"

"You're welcome Brittany, now hook my shit up, the Heat are in town tonight and I gotta be looking right so they can tip a bitch!"

"You know I'm going to have you looking 100. How's everybody doing?"

"They cool baby, still shaking and whatever else. Oh you

21

know your ex-boyfriend's homeboy got married too!"

"Who?"

"The one with the detail shop over in Buckhead!"

"Oh Rich! Damn I need to call my girl and congratulate her."

"How is she your girl and you ain't go to the wedding?"

"Well, she's kinda my girl, we really only hung out a few times with Kev and Rich."

"Ummm hmmm, I heard she was a fine ass ho too!"

"She alright."

"Will you hit?"

"What?"

"Girl this is Blu you're talking to! I said will you hit?"

"I ain't even gone lie Blu, she can get it!"

"Ha-ha! Britt you still a fool!"

As Blu leans back for her rinse, Brittany couldn't help but to think about the time she spent with Kev.

"Damn bitch!"

"Oh shit! I'm sorry Blu, I didn't mean to spray you in your eye." She smirks.

"Brittany, that's why I aint tipping your ass. You're day

23

dreaming about that girl ain't you!"

"What! Shut your butt up and lean back!"

"Hey be careful girl, you know I bruise easy. I don't need to hear J-Rocks damn mouth. You know how he is."

"Are you still fucking that fool?"

"Yep and as long as he's paying my bills and giving a bitch free tip out, I'm gone keep screwing him."

"Blu, you're a mess!"

"Whatever, just finish my hair Melissa, don't trip."

ANTWAN BANK$

"I ain't tripping Blu, that's your business."

"Good, now let's talk about something else, like when are you coming to do a set?"

"Blu, please! Just hush your mouth and let me finish your hair."

―――――――――

The warm, Atlanta sun beamed through the panoramic windows on the 28th floor of Rich's high rise condo as the shadows from the surrounding skyline forecast over their white leather furniture. The two way mirror windows mask the newly-weds as they parade around in their birthday suits.

Another day dawns, but this one was different from all of those that came before.

"What do you want for breakfast hun?"

"Whatever you cook Mrs. Blackmon!"

"Well, I was thinking about making some Captain Crunch!"

"Don't start tripping Melissa; I want some eggs, bacon, grits and toast!"

"Who's going to cook that?"

Ring-Ring! Ring-Ring!

"Woman I'm going to throw that damn phone in the garbage!"

"You're not, crazy!"

Ring-Ring! Rich picks the phone up off the kitchen counter and looks at it.

"It's Brittany!"

"Who?"

"Kevin's ex!"

"Oh, let me have it."

Rich hands Melissa the phone then walks over to the fridge.

"Hello!"

"Congratulations girl!"

"Thank you, Brittany!"

"You're welcome and why didn't I get an invitation?"

"I did send one for you and Kev, but I didn't know you two had broken up."

"Yeah, that's over, but I'm happy that you guys are married. Are you excited?"

"Girl, you know Kev brought some chic named Sybil to the wedding right?"

"What the fuck did you just say?"

"I think Rich said her name was Sybil. Hold on! Rich!"

"Yeah baby, what's up?"

"What was that girl's name that Kev brought to the wedding?"

"I don't know!"

"See, why are you lying?! Brittany now he's talking about he doesn't know; I'm sure her name was Sybil."

"Umm hmm, I know that bitch."

"Well, we're about to eat breakfast then finish packing so we can go on our honey moon. I will come by the shop when we get back in town."

"Alright Melissa and where are you guys going?"

"We're flying to Dubai."

"Damn, now that's a honeymoon!"

"Brittany you're silly, I'll tell you all about it when we return."

"Ok, have fun and tell Rich I said congratulations."

"Alright Brittany, I sure will."

"Why did you tell that woman about Sybil?"

"What?"

"Melissa you're about to put yourself in the middle of a storm, don't say I didn't warn you."

"Calm down Rich, Brittany is a big girl. I'm sure she's over Kev by now."

30

"I don't know baby, but I sure hope so or you're going to be caught up in it."

"Mr. Blackmon, do I look worried?"

"No you don't Mrs. Blackmon."

"Alright then!"

Honeymoon

A steady flow of cars make their way onto the lot of Rich's Buckhead Body car wash. Joyce, the shop receptionist greets the customers as they pull up to take their place in line. Her silky black hair was naturally curled up just above her shoulders. She wipes the sweat from her brow as one car pulls off the lot and another enters.

"Joyce, wait a few minutes before you send the next one into the bay. The fellas need to restock their chemicals and sponges."

"Alright Rock, you're going to have to do this. It's too freaking hot, I'm going back to my desk."

"Hey girl, you got 10 minutes and I need you back out here collecting this money."

"Boy, don't make me curse your ass out!"

"Joyce! Joyce!"

"I'm going inside Rock, you do it!"

Rock, the shop manager looks over the lot to gather where all his employees were. The short stocky brother from Brooklyn earned his nickname because of his hardcore demeanor. Let's just say he wasn't shy about laying his hands on you.

"Man this chick gone make me pimp slap her today."

"I heard that Rock!"

"Heard what? I ain't say nothing."

Rock walks away from the entrance then over towards the crew of employees waxing a black hummer.

"Hey, yall got this baby looking good son!"

"Thanks Rock!"

"Yeah no doubt, make sure you guys put one of those trees

with the new car scent up in this baby."

"Alright we got it."

Ring-Ring! Ring-Ring!

"Hello, thanks for calling The Buckhead Body Wash. How can I help you?"

"Yes, I was calling to see if my car was ready yet?"

"Sure what kind of car do you have, Sir?"

"It's the black F-150 with the all black rims."

"Oh yes, it's been done for an hour now, sugar."

"Thanks baby, I'm on the way."

"You're welcome!"

Joyce hangs up the phone then looks around the lobby area to see if anyone was waiting inside. After a quick glance she realizes that she's all alone.

Ding! The cash register drawer opens. Nervously but quickly she reaches inside and snatches a few twenties, tens and five dollar bills from its grasp. Ring-Ring! Ring-Ring!

"Oh shit!"

The phone startles her as she stuffs the stolen money into her C cup bra. Ring-Ring! Ring-

Ring! Joyce calms down and clears her throat as she picks up the phone.

"Um-Um! Hello, thanks for calling-"

"Joyce it's me, where is Rock?"

"Oh hey Boss, he's on the lot."

"Alright I was just calling to let you guys know that Melissa and I are leaving for Dubai in a few hours. If you need to reach me call Melissa's cell phone, my battery is dead."

"Ok Rich, I'll let Rock know and you guys have a good trip."

"Thanks Joyce, you two hold it down for me and don't be coming in late to work either."

"Man I'm always on time Boss."

"Joyce save it, I'll see ya'll when we get back."

"Ok bye!"

Excitement flows through Rich's physique as he leans against his kitchen counter admiring the Atlanta skyline through his large windows. The soft fragrance of Dolce & Gabbana tingles his senses as Melissa walks towards him.

"Hun, can you zip me up?"

"Sure!"

She slowly turns her back to Rich then lifts her hair up off her soft shoulders. Melissa's bronze skin complimented the white strapless knee high Vera Wang dress she wore as Rich seductively zips it up from the back.

"Thanks honey, I'm all packed and ready to go. What time is the driver coming?"

"He should be here any minute!"

"Great. I am so excited, we really need this trip."

"You sure are looking delicious Mrs. Blackmon, come over here and let me taste you."

"Is that all you think about Richard, fucking?"

"No, but right now I want to lift your ass up onto that counter, spread those creamy thighs then lick your funky emotions!"

"Well, can we save it for Dubai?"

"Save it? Woman I have plenty to go around and I'm not running out any time soon."

Rich forces his muscular frame against hers simultaneously pushing her back up against the warm window pane. He places both hands around her waist, slides her up the glass while she moans and opens her legs.

"Ummm! Rich what are you doing."

"Shut up Melissa and give me my pussy."

Her legs now wrapped around his neck while the back of her shoulders brace firmly against the window pane. Rich begins licking her sugar walls like a vanilla ice cream cone on a hot summer day. Bam-Bam! Bam-Bam!

"Wait hun, someone is at the door."

"God dammit, who is it!?"

"I'm your driver sir, do you guys have any bags that you need me to get."

"Ugh! It was getting good too hun."

"Yeah whatever, we'll finish this later!"

"That's what I told you anyway."

Bam-Bam! Bam-Bam!

"I'm coming man, hold your horses."

"Baby, make sure we got everything, Dubai is a long way from home."

As Rich finally makes his way to the door, Melissa picks up

her phone and scrolls through some new text messages that she just received from her work number.

"Hi Melissa, I hope that you enjoy your trip to Dubai. See you later."

She looks up to see where Rich was then quickly responds back with an auto reply.

"Thank you!"

As Rich and the driver took the bags out to the car Melissa did one last walk through to assure that they had gotten everything. She turns the lamp on by the sofa and tunes the radio station to V103 before leaving. Buzz-Buzz! Just as she locks the door another text alert comes through.

"I'm going to miss you Melissa; how long are you going to be gone?"

"Bill you need to chill, you're starting to worry me." She replied.

"I'm serious!"

"Look, I'm on the way to the airport; I'll text you when I get some time!"

"Ok!" Bill replied.

"Hey did you lock up?"

"Yep, we're all good Rich!"

"Cool baby, now let's get to Hartsfield! Dubai, awaits us!"

Melissa gazes out the window during the entire drive while Rich kicks back looking up through the sun roof of the limo puffing on his acid cigar.

"What's wrong baby, are you alright?"

"Yeah, just don't feel like smelling that stinky cigar."

"We're going to be on that plane for 15 hours, I'm getting my smoke on right now, so roll the window down or something."

"Nah, I'll be fine, smoke your cigar."

Thirty minutes of awkward silence pass before they finally arrive at the terminal amidst the busy Atlanta airport traffic. The driver pulls over to the curb, parks then proceeds to remove the luggage for boarding. Buzz-Buzz! Melissa receives another text alert as Rich puffs on his cigar while looking over at her.

"Are you going to see who that is?"

"It's probably work."

"Well, don't you think you need to check it and tell them that you won't be available for a few days? Oh and I told the guys at the shop to call your cell if they needed to reach me too."

"Why did you do that?"

"Because I don't think my phone is going to have a signal over there."

"Baby you have Sprint, I'm sure that your phone can take international calls. If it doesn't then you need to drop their ass."

Buzz-Buzz! Melissa reluctantly looks down at her phone then checks the incoming text.

"Melissa!" Bill messages.

Beep! She shuts off her phone, slides it in her purse then gets out of the limo. Rich follows, drops his cigar by the curb then joins his wife inside the airport. He notices she turned off her phone but hesitates to say something, maybe she was tired of the office calling he thought to himself. Rich grabs his wife around the waist as they approach check in.

———————————

Fifteen hours into the flight the couple finds themselves over the Arabian Sea. Tired and restless, Rich holds his wife by her cheeks and kisses her on the lips as she stares into his eyes in awe of his affection.

"Ladies and gentlemen this is your pilot speaking. If you look over to your left you can see the Palm Islands below, off to the right is the island of Jumierah."

"Wow, that's gorgeous hun, isn't it?"

"Sure is and I can't wait to make love to you on the balcony overlooking all that water!"

"That's the only thing on your mind I see."

"Melissa it's our honeymoon, it should be on your mind too."

"Yeah but not like yours, you horny toad."

"Girl, the way that I'm feeling you might get pregnant while we're over here."

"Not! Where are we staying?"

"We're staying at The Atlantis and what do you mean not?"

"Um."

Melissa grunts at the mention of the Atlantis hotel. Rich had no idea that this was not the first time his wife found herself visiting Palm Island.

"Ladies and gentlemen thank you for flying Delta it's now 105 degrees in Dubai. We will be landing shortly so please make sure that your seat belts are fastened and your chairs are in their upright positions."

"Hey woman, I said what do you mean by not?"

"I'm not ready for a baby Rich, let's just enjoy our trip and we can discuss babies later, is that ok?"

"Sure. No problem."

The heat from the desert felt thick and humid as Melissa and Rich found themselves fighting to stay cool while they waited on the sidewalk for their limo to arrive. An array of spices consumes the warm air, a combination unlike any back in the States. Different shades of brown skinned citizens and visitors alike congest the vehicle waiting area.

"Man it smells like one of those Indian restaurants out here, doesn't it baby?"

"That's because we are what we eat hun, you're smelling culture."

"Damn, I don't want to know what America smells like then."

"Ha-ha! Rich you're crazy, why you say that?"

"Melissa we eat so many different things in America, it has to smell bad."

"It actually smells like beef when you land in America."

"I bet it does! Look here's our ride."

Images of sky scrapers amidst the Arabian Sea mirror in the black limo paint and tinted windows as it rolls up in front of the couple. The white Atlantis Palm Island logo lay claim to the center window as the car came to a stop.

"Hello Mr. and Mrs. Blackmon I presume?"

"Yes sir, that is correct."

"Sorry Sir that I am late, but the traffic is a little crazy today, we have several conventions in town."

"Yeah ok, can you get our bags please, it's hot as hell out here."

"Yes ma'am!"

The view of the massive sea along with the beautiful skyline becomes overwhelming the closer that they get. Heat waves rise above the hot concrete making the castle Atlantis blurry in the distance as the limo approaches Jumierah, Palm Island.

"Ok my friends, we have arrived. Welcome to Atlantis."

Breathtaking beauty like no other stood larger than life as

the newly-weds look on in amusement. A 50 foot arch way welcomes them at the entrance as the bell hop escorts the couple into a world of Arabian luxury. Decorative marble floors blanket the lobby area which was also home to immense art décor, palm tree pillars standing 100 feet tall and a huge blue crystal like tree with a flowing waterfall that held the center of attention.

"Now, if this doesn't make you want to have a baby then-

"Rich come on and let's just check in hun, I'm beat!"

"Hello and welcome to Atlantis at Palm Island. May I have your name, please?"

"Yes, I'm Richard Blackmon and I have a reservation for two."

"Ok sir, I have you here, will you be using the American Express on file?"

"Yeah, that's fine ma'am."

"That is good, so here are two keys for you and your wife. Jahir will be escorting you nice people upstairs to your Grand Atlantis Suite."

"Alright thank you, baby."

"How much did you spend on that suite Rich?"

"Lissa stop being a financial advisor for once and just enjoy the moment. I'm not hurting for money, so chill ok."

"I just don't want you to over-do it, Rich, that's all."

Soon, as they exit the elevator, Rich stops in the middle of the hallway as the bellhop is opening the suite door. He places his hands around Melissa's waist then looks her in the eyes.

"I've been meaning to tell you this, but now is as good a time as any I guess."

57

"What is it?"

"Well, Kev put me on to this shopping mall deal down in Myrtle Beach and I just closed on it about a week ago."

"Honey, why didn't you-"

"Ok Sir, Madam this is your room and I will be here for a few more hours, please let me know if you need anything."

"Thank you Jahir! Lissa give him a tip."

She reaches in her purse then pulls two crisp twenty dollar bills from the inside pocket.

"Thank you very much Ma'am!"

"You're welcome! Now what were you saying Rich?"

"I flipped a shopping mall and it has the potential to make millions."

"I really wish you would have consulted with me first before doing that."

"Come here woman!"

Bam! He slams the door shut, pulls off his shirt then pulls Mrs. Blackmon in close. Inside she felt her juices flowing not because of the physical contact but from the thought of the potential million dollar deal her husband just closed.

If there was any doubt about why she married Rich that news alone made her remember why she fell in love with him in the first place. He was a convict with a few degrees, owned a successful detail shop that garnered six figures and he had the business savvy of Donald Trump.

The Arabian print rugs, plush furniture, antique lamps and high dollar art pieces only serve as background during their most intimate moment yet. Rip! He snatches the Vera Wang from her caramel toned body and leaves her naked standing in heels alone. A cool breeze blew in off the Arabian Sea through the balcony doors standing ajar as they move towards its opening. Melissa found herself holding each side of the doorway while she faced the sky blue sea, her naked ass arched up high begging for attention.

Richard slips off his pants and moves in closer to his wife. Her hair blew flawlessly in the wind while he slowly licked the nape of her neck then down her fragile spinal-cord. Sensuous moans exude from Lissa's diaphragm as she anticipates his tongue down the crack of her-

"Ohhh Rich! Ohhh Rich! Ohhh Rich!"

She yells with every long stroke that penetrates her sugar walls. He grabs her by the waist then proceeds to repeatedly slide his black love inside her throbbing womb.

Seconds turn to minutes, ten minutes turn to twenty then to thirty.

"Oh my God, I love you nigga, damn!"

"What, I can't hear you? Say it again!"

"I love you, Rich! I fucking love you!"

Satisfied that he'd just done what he was yearning for, Rich smacks his wife on the ass while she's having her orgasm. He was sure that he just made a baby while making love overlooking the Arabian Sea.

"Damn that was good, I need a drink now hun."

"I can use one too baby."

Rich walks over to their bags, picks up a few and takes them into the bedroom.

"Wow, you have to see this room Melissa!"

"Ok, I'm coming!"

Lissa picks up her purse to check her phone for any messages. She turns it on and finds several missed incoming texts from Mr. Kennedy.

"Melissa, I'm at the Atlantis, I know you're staying here. Meet me down stairs in the lobby."

"What the *fuck*, Bill!?" She replied.

"What took you so long, come meet me!" He responds.

Irate, she paces back and forth trying to come up with a plan. This had all the signs of a disaster. Never in her wildest dreams could she have imagined that Bill would follow her to Dubai.

"Hun, I'm going downstairs to get us some drinks. They don't have any good vodka in the liquor cabinet."

"Alright, see if they have some Cohiba's too."

"What?"

"Cigar's baby!"

"Oh ok, I'll be back in a minute!"

"Alright!"

Melissa hastily grabs Rich's gym bag off the floor and finds a T-Shirt and shorts to slip on. She hurries out the door

65

barefooted and fired up while texting Bill.

"Meet me at the bar!"

"Ok," he replied.

She exits the elevator then pauses for a second to let the adrenalin settle and catches her breath before entering the bar. And, there he was. William, with his tall white frame, tapered blonde hair and blue eyes sat at the end of the bar like everything was normal. He and his blue Brooks Brothers suit fit in perfectly among the business elite that were patronizing the bar this evening.

"Dude, you can't be serious! Why are you even here?"

"Calm down Melissa, I can explain."

"God dammit, get to it."

"John had to meet a new oil client here but he got ill, so I came in his place."

"That's bullshit, Bill!"

"I'm serious baby, you being here only made the trip that much sweeter."

"Bill this is not the time or place, I am on my honeymoon. Do you understand that my husband is just upstairs! Can you comprehend that?"

"I hear you loud and clear, but you don't love him because if you did, you would've never come to meet me."

Ring-Ring!

"Dammit! Dammit!"

"What's wrong?"

"It's my husband calling." Ring-Ring!

Melissa looks down at the phone and before she knew it she inadvertently taps the ignore button. Ring-Ring! Ring-Ring! Rich calls again.

"Bill I have to go and please do not call me again. I'll see you back in the States."

William jumps up from the bar then grabs Melissa by the arm.

"Wait!"

Ring-Ring! Ring-Ring! Her heart starts beating at an alarming rate as she literally stood torn in between two lovers. One her new husband the other her forbidden office affair. Melissa knew Rich well enough to know that shit was about to get real. She hadn't answered any of his calls and it was time for her to get going or come up with some quick answers, but Bill wasn't moving. Ring-Ring! Ring-Ring!

"Stay with me tonight!"

"Fool, are you crazy? You're about to get both of us killed."

"I love you Melissa."

"God help me! Bill, please go!"

Ring-Ring!   Ring-Ring!   He refuses to leave her side as the phone continues to ring.

Trust

Rich pulls the phone away from his ear and looks to see if he was indeed calling his wife. Then for what seemed like the third time his call went to voicemail. An acute nervousness consumes his soul as all kind of thoughts cross his mind. Before he knew it, he was in the hallway barefooted, buttoning his pants and slipping on his shirt while in route down to the lobby.

He decides to call again as he approaches the lobby entrance. Ring-Ring! Ring-Ring! Melissa in a frantic jerks her arm away from Bill.

"Bill I have to go! You're going to get us both killed!" Ring-Ring! Ring-Ring!

"Melissa, wait!"

William yells out to Lissa as she pulls away just as she attempts to answer her phone, but there was Rich standing there watching it all unfold.

"Who the fuck is that and why aren't you answering your phone?"

"Hey hun, oh that was one of my colleagues from our Asian Office. We met during that convention in Chicago."

"What's his name?"

"Mr. Kennedy, he's my boss's nephew."

Rich turns to his left and stares at Bill as he disappears in the distance across the marble floor and amidst the stunning décor. This left a funny feeling in his gut, but he couldn't put his finger on why; he just took notice.

"So why didn't you answer your phone?"

"My phone didn't ring!"

"Yo don't start that bullshit. I called you at least 4 times. Let me see that damn phone!"

Abruptly he snatches her cell away from her grasp.

"Rich!"

"Shut up Lissa!"

"Boy you trippin'!"

Rich slides the home screen to search her calls, but the phone was locked.

"Here, unlock this shit!"

"Ugh, let me hold it! See look no missed calls."

"Yeah whatever, that's because you sent them to voicemail."

Rich pauses then gives Melissa one of those 'I'm gone fuck you up' looks. He knew something was up. She grabs his unbuttoned shirt and pulls him in close to her.

"Honey its ok, why were you calling anyway?"

"I need a lighter!"

"Well come on, let's go get one from the shop. I didn't even have time to get our drinks before Mr. Kennedy stopped me."

_____

Meanwhile back in the ATL, the heat index was at a real feel of 105 degrees as the cars piled one behind the other awaiting their Saturday wax jobs at

Rich's detail shop. Kevin pulls on the lot and bypasses all the waiting cars then parks his blue Maserati by the office in front of Rock while he's puffing on a Newport.

"Kev, my nigga, what's up son?"

"What's poppin Rock! I need this baby shined up."

"No doubt, just leave it right there, I'll get the boys to jump on it next."

"Thanks Rock, it's hotter than hell out here. Is there some cold water inside?"

"Yeah man, just ask Joyce for a bottle, she has some in the fridge behind the counter."

"Alright bet!"

The cool breeze from the AC was a welcoming feeling as it smacked Kev in the face as soon as he walked inside. Young Jeezy's raspy voice is playing over the shop speakers from the Hot 107.9 radio waves. Several patrons occupy the lobby watching the flat screen TVs while they wait on their rides as Joyce sits behind the counter in all her beauty.

Before Kevin approaches the front desk he stops and waits by the window for Joyce to complete her transaction with a customer.

"Your total will be $58.90, Sir."

"Here you go lovely lady and you keep the change for yourself."

The gentleman gives Joyce three crisp 20 dollar bills and one 5 dollar bill.

"Oh thank you sugar!"

"You're welcome and I'll see you next weekend."

"Ok, you enjoy the rest of your weekend too!"

"I sure will, thanks again Joyce."

Complacent, Joyce does like she's done so many times before; she folds up the $65 then slides it in her bra. Kev notices this and can't believe what he just saw. He couldn't help but to wonder how often Joyce has been stealing Rich's money. Just then Kev decides to take a seat and monitor her actions for a while.

He finds himself sitting through at least 4 more transactions and sure enough she pockets at least three out of four for herself. Appalled at what he just witnessed Kev reluctantly walks up to the counter to retrieve that bottle of water.

"Hello Joyce!"

"Hey Kevin, isn't it?"

"Yep, that's me."

"How are you?"

"I'm a little thirsty; Rock said you had some cold water back here."

"Sure, you want one?"

"Please."

"Here you go, sugar. You know Rich is out of town right?"

"Yeah, when is he coming back?"

"I think they're coming back tomorrow, he's been gone for 3 days already."

"Ok thanks, you have a nice day Joyce."

"You're welcome Kev and you do the same."

Even though the temperature exceeded 100 degrees he walks outside, retrieves his cell then calls Rich. The phone rings several times before he finally answers.

"Hello!"

"Hey who is this?"

"It's Kevin, man."

"Oh, hey bruh, the damn caller ID said unknown number."

"Are you still in Dubai?"

"Yeah, we're at the airport now."

"Cool, hit me up when you get back to the A. We need to talk about some things."

"Alright no problem, is everything good, bruh?"

Kev remains silent for a few seconds before he finally answers his friend.

"Kev?"

"Everything is good my nigga, I just want to speak with you

about some more financial opportunities."

"Bet! I'm all about that coin, bruh and did you hear anything about my Myrtle Beach property?"

"It's doing well. My property manager says that the office has been receiving calls about leasing the units."

"Cool, I'll call you tomorrow. Where do you want to meet?"

"Let's hit the Run and Shoot, get a few games in."

"See you there bruh, how's 6 O'clock?"

"That'll work Rich, have a safe trip."

"Thanks man, later."

Well rested and back to work, Melissa enters the elevator of her firm's office then checks her reflection in the gold plated doors while she stands there all alone. She takes a deep breath and tries to shake off the jetlag before the elevator reaches the 55th floor. Images of Bill and Rich play over and over in her mind's eye as the doors slide open.

As she exits the elevator, butterflies thump the walls of her stomach during every step. The firm's executive assistant smiles and welcomes Mrs. Blackmon back to work upon her arrival.

"Welcome back Melissa! How was your honeymoon? I want to hear all about it!"

"It was lovely Ingrid and I can't wait to tell you how much fun I had."

"Awesome sauce! So you'll tell me at lunch then?"

"Yes Ingrid."

Lissa gazed down the narrow hallway for a sign of her boss, but there was no sign of him. His car was in its regular space when she parked so he was here somewhere she thought to herself. The sweet smell of flowers met Melissa at her corner office entrance. A bright smile donned her face as she got closer to the desk that held a bouquet of purple lilies.

She reaches for the card to see who sent them, but it was blank and she had an idea who. The smoke grey freshly vacuumed plush carpet held clues of size eleven foot prints that trotted from the door to her cherry oak desk. Ring-Ring! Ring-Ring! Melissa hastily takes her seat behind the huge desk. Ring-Ring!

"Yes Ingrid?"

"Mr. Wallace from Dallas Incorporated is on line one."

"Ok you can transfer it; I guess it's back to work now, huh?"

""Yes Ma'am, I guess so. Here's Mr. Wallace."

"Hello Mr. Wallace; thanks for holding- What the fu-

"Excuse me!"

Melissa jumps up from her seat in shock from five white fingers that found their way up her dress. Bill let out a huge laugh to her reaction, but he was the only one amused.

"William Kennedy if you don't get your crazy ass out of my office!"

Ingrid runs to see what all of the commotion was about.

"Mrs. Blackmon is everything ok!"

"Yes Ingrid, can you close my door please!"

"Yes Ma'am."

"Bill, are you fucking crazy?"

"Yep, I'm crazy about you."

Lissa stares at Bill as he stands to his feet. She knew this was going to be a problem. It was only a matter of time before this thing between them was going to blow. Reality had just sunk in and it was that William Kennedy with all of his corporate accolades was indeed a nut.

"Look Bill, we need to have a talk. How about we go to Houston's after work and discuss some things."

"Sure, no problem and you better take care of Mr. Wallace; I think he's still on the phone."

"Dammit! Hello Mr. Wallace, are you still there?"

"Yes Ma'am, what in heaven's name is going on over there? Was that Bill's voice I heard?"

"No Sir, a spider was on my desk and I'm scared to death of spiders. Now where were we?"

She tried with all her might to concentrate, but there was no need. Melissa knew the affair with Bill was a ticking time bomb and she needed to diffuse it before Rich caught on or else.

Dark clouds overcast the Atlanta mid-day sky as Kev cruised onto the gym lot gazing over it slowly for any sign of Rich.

"Kev! Kev!"

Kevin stops the car to locate the voice that was screaming

out his name. He looks right then left and finally in the rear view to find Rich sitting on the trunk of his Porsche.

"I see you playa, let me park!" He yells out.

The air was humid and smelled of rain, but the forecast didn't call for showers. Rich looks up at the dark sky for a second then picks up his bag and walks towards Kev while he contemplated the outcome of the weather.

"What's up bruh, how was Dubai?"

"Man that place is unbelievable!"

"Yeah I heard it was; I'm going to have to take a trip over there."

"Yep do that! So what's good, are you ready to go run this court?"

"In a minute, I need to talk to you about something."

"Man, don't tell me you done went off and got married or something!"

"Nah man, this is serious though."

Rich sits his bag on the ground beside the Maserati. He didn't like the look on Kevin's face and that concerned him.

"Kev what's up?"

"How long have you known Joyce?"

"Who?"

"You're receptionist!"

"I've known her for a few years or so. Why you ask?"

Kev leans back against his car door as he starts to explain.

"Bro, I went to your spot the other day to get my car waxed and something caught my attention."

"What day was this and what caught your attention?"

"It was the day I called you when you were at the airport."

"Ok, go on…"

Rich was all ears, he had a bad feeling in his gut about the words that were about to come out of Kevin's mouth.

"Well, I went inside to get a bottle of water from Joyce, but when I walked in she had a customer at the counter, so I waited."

Light rain drops begin to fall at a slow pace as the two friends continue to talk.

"So the customer pays her like $65 if I'm not mistaken. The bill came to $55 I think and he gave her a $10 tip."

"Alright that's normal, she's a nice looking girl and guys often tip her well."

"Hold on Rich, I'm not done."

"My bad, go ahead."

"So once the guy walks away, Joyce takes the $65 and stashes it in her bra."

"What!"

"You heard me man, and she did it three more times out of the next four customers you had."

"Are you sure?"

"Positive!"

"I'm going to drag that bitch!"

"Yo calm down, don't go do anything crazy Rich. Think about this for a minute before you act man."

"Ain't no thinking to be done Kev, this ho is stealing from me!"

"Don't you have some cameras at the shop?"

"Yeah there's a few!"

"So just watch them and see for yourself, that way when you approach her you'll have evidence."

"Yo I need to go handle this shit bruh, I ain't in the mood to shoot no ball."

"I understand my dude; let me know if you need my help."

"Thanks for telling me Kev; I'll get at you."

Rich gives his friend a pound and makes his way back to the car. Disappointment, shock and anger overtake his soul as he ponders his next move. The loud sounds from burning rubber, along with clouds of white smoke permeate the air as the white Porsche fish tales off the lot.

Real Love

Steaming inside he pulls into a handicap parking space in the front of Melissa's building. Heavy drops of rain dance on the hot pavement as he calmly steps out of his car, with his clothes soaking wet and dripping with water Rich walks inside to go find his wife.

His soaked Jordan's squeak with every step and leave a trail of wet shoe-prints in route to the elevator. Every bone in Rich's body wanted to go find Joyce and rip her a new asshole, but he figured some time with his wife would calm his nerves.

He wipes the rain water from his forehead as he looks into the gold plated elevator doors just before it stopped on her office floor.

"Hello Sir, how may I help you?"

"Yes. I'm here to see my wife!"

"And who is your wife, Sir?"

"Mrs. Blackmon."

"Oh Hello, I'm Ingrid, nice to meet you!"

"Yeah, where's her office?"

"It's the third door on your right Mr. Blackmon."

"Thanks Ingrid-

"Ingrid I'll be in the conference room if you need me!" A voice interrupted.

"Ok Mr. Kennedy!"

Rich stood in silence as the tall white male leaned over the corner of Ingrid's desk. A feeling of Deja' Vu had come over him; something about the gentleman seemed strangely familiar.

"Oh Mr. Kennedy, this is Mr. Blackmon, Melissa's husband."

Bill looks at Rich and gives him a smile and a nod. Rich obliges just as William turns and walks away.

"Say Ingrid, that guy looks familiar, I saw someone that resembled him when Melissa and I were in Dubai."

"Dubai, hmmm that could have been him, we have an office in Asia and the agents do frequent Dubai often."

"Oh really, was Mr. Kennedy over there last week?"

"Yes I think so, Mr. Blackmon."

"Bill wouldn't happen to have a nephew that works over in Asia, would he?"

"No that's nonsense, Mr. Kennedy is an only child, he doesn't have any nephews."

Rich stood quiet for a moment and thought back on that night he saw Melissa and the gentleman at the bar.

"Mr. Blackmon, are you ok?"

"Yes I'm sorry, where did you say Melissa's office was again?"

Rich, full of emotions and not to mention soaking wet makes his way to his wife's office.

"Honey, what are you doing here?"

"Hey baby, we need to talk."

Melissa is taken aback; it wasn't like Rich to show up at her job. She gathers herself and carries on.

"Come in and sit down... look at you, you're all wet and sticky looking."

"Yeah, this isn't even half of my problems."

"What's wrong?"

She sits on the edge of her brown leather couch juxtapose to Rich.

"I just left Kev at the gym and he told me some bad news."

"Oh my God, is everything ok?"

"Nah, he caught that bitch Joyce stealing from me."

"What!?"

"You heard me baby."

"When did this happen?"

"Just the other day! We were at the airport!"

"Oh, I remember you were on the phone with him."

"Yeah, he knew then but waited to tell me."

Melissa tries to comfort Rich by rubbing his leg with her left hand and holding his hand with the other as she faces him.

"So what are you going to do hun?"

"I'm going to stop by the shop once I leave here so I can look at the security tapes. Maybe I'll do it in the morning, I don't know."

"Don't do anything crazy now."

"I'm good Melissa; I just needed to cool off before I went over there."

"Ok, I'm glad you stopped by. Oh, Brittany called."

"What did she want?"

"She invited me out for drinks tomorrow after work at Six Feet Under."

"So that's your new buddy now?"

"Rich chill, she just wants to hang out."

"Alright don't get fucked up, Kev told me she was trifling."

"Rich!"

"What?"

"Be nice."

"I'm just saying. Don't make this a habit."

"I won't. I promise." Muah-

Melissa kisses Rich on the left cheek as he stands to his feet.

"I'll see you at home in a few baby, let me go handle this thief."

"Yes sir and did you want me to pick up something to eat when I leave the office?"

"Nah, I'll grab some Popeye's on the way to the shop."

"Ok hun, later!"

Bright sun rays illuminated the downstairs lobby as if not a drop of rain fell from the sky just an hour ago. Rich reaches for his cell as he's walking outside to his car that was conveniently parked in the handicap zone and calls Rock.

"Hey Boss, what's up?"

"Rock, are you still at the shop?"

"Yeah, I was about to leave until J-Rock called me to clean his damn limo."

"Cool, I'll be there in 15 minutes; we need to have a conversation."

"Is everything ok Rich?"

"Shit, that's what I need to talk to you about."

"Alright, me and the twins will be here cleaning the limo."

"Just stay there, I'll see you in a bit."

Blu and J-Rock exit the black stretched navigator and make their way into the lobby.

"New York, how long is it going to take you man? We need to pick up some Houston dancers from Hartsfield in about two hours."

J-Rock could never bring himself to call Rock, Rock. He for some stupid reason thought that he owned the name so he always used New York instead.

"We'll be done way before then, son!"

"Cool, where's Rich? That nigga ain't never at his own place of business."

"He's on the way."

"Bet and when are you fools coming to spend some of this hard earned cash at Club Ebony?"

"Whenever you get some sexy girls in that bitch."

"Excuse me fool! What are you trying to say?"

"I just said it red!"

"First of all my name ain't Red, it's Blu!"

Rock nonchalantly walks away from what looks to be a losing battle and proceeds to help the twins clean the limo.

"Blu, calm your ass down, ain't no need for all of this damn drama."

"Oh, you didn't hear him call your girls ugly!"

"Shit, some of y'all hoes is ugly! I mean you're fine, but you know good and damn well that it's a few butta heads in the crew."

"Butta heads?"

"Yep, everything looks good but her head!" J-Rock starts to laugh at his own joke.

"Aww whatever, you got that joke from Shawty-Shawty, you ain't funny."

Errrrr! Rich pulls onto the lot at a high speed and comes to an abrupt stop with tires screeching. J-Rock and Blu stop at the lobby entrance admiring the cocaine white Porsche as he exits.

"Yo Rock, come holler at me, let the twins finish that shit!"

Rock looks at Rich with a confused look but follows him into the office.

"Excuse me, J-Rock we need to get in the office."

"Oh, my bad Rich! Blu come on baby let's go smoke this blunt!"

Rock nervously walks in step with his employer until they reach his office.

"Come in and have a seat Rock."

"Bro what's going on? I've never seen you this upset!"

"Tell me you didn't know that Joyce was robbing me!"

"What?"

New York stands there in shock and can't believe the words that are leaving Rich's mouth.

"Hold on, if she is I don't know anything about it."

"Well she is!"

"Those are some very serious accusations boss man, do you have any proof?"

"Yeah as a matter of fact I do."

"What proof, you got her on tape or something because you know she's going to deny it until her last breath."

"Kev saw her with his own eyes and he doesn't have any reason to make that shit up."

"Man you know we're like a family around here, so I think you should talk to her first to hear what she has to say."

Rich walks over to the security monitor in his office then taps the rewind button.

"This will tell me all I need to know Rock."

Knock-Knock!

"Yeah who is it?"

"It's J-Rock, Rich."

"I'm busy man, what do you need?"

"Yo the twins are finished with the limo; they told us to come pay you."

"Alright Jay, just give it to Rock."

Rock walks over to the door and takes the cash from Jay as Blu curiously scopes the office from the entrance.

"Thanks for looking out too Rich, the first round is on me whenever you guys come to Ebony."

"No problem bro, we may take you up on that offer too."

Rock takes a seat on the office couch, leans forward then places both elbows on his knees with his fingers interlocked, forearms extended as they held up his chin. He and Rich watch in awe as the cameras obviously show Joyce indeed stealing cash from the business.

"Damn, that's fucked up boss. What are you going to do?"

"First I'm going to have a face to face with her then I'll probably kill her."

"Whoa! Don't do anything crazy Rich, let's call it a night

and you can handle this thing with a clear head tomorrow."

"Yeah, I'm going home to get me some head and fuck my wife until we fall asleep. This situation has me stressed, I still can't believe it."

Later the next day empty Stella Artois bottles, soiled bed sheets, empty Popeye's boxes and wine glasses show proof of a night's past. Rich lay in their King size bed, head throbbing and stomach growling as he glances at the clock that reads 4:55 PM.

He tries to sit up, but the throbbing in his skull knocked

him back down at every attempt until he surrenders to its painful raft. The soft smell of Dolce & Gabbana perfume was the only presence of Melissa. In denial he shouts out her name.

"Melissa! Melissa, I'm hungry!"

He shouts and shouts but no Lissa. Rich picks up his cell phone from the floor and speed dials his wife.

"Hello hun."

"Baby where are you?"

"I'm about to meet Brittany at Six Feet Under. I told you don't you remember?"

"No, I don't but my damn head is killing me and I'm starving."

"Well it was worth it, we never made love that long before, we got three hours in last night!"

"Damn, no wonder I'm drained."

"Yep, but I have to go; I'll bring you something to eat when I leave."

"Thanks Melissa!"

"Yep, bye hun!'

Melissa was really excited to finally sit down and talk with Brittany. This would be the first time that the two have seen each other since the cook out over at Kevin's months ago. She finds a park behind the building then makes her way into the restaurant.

Dim lighting mask the loud patrons dressed in their Braves jerseys, hats and T-Shirts as they enjoy a quick bite just hours before the game at Turner Field. Commentators analyze past and present games on the overhead flat screens as loud chatter echoes throughout the dining area. Brittany slowly walks back and forth in front of the door waiting for Melissa to enter.

"Hey girl, I am starving, what took you so long?"

"Child I was on the phone with my husband, he's going through it right now."

"Why, what's wrong?"

"Your ex told him that his shop receptionist was stealing from him."

"Damn, I swear Kev just needs to mind his business sometimes."

"No he was right to tell Rich about it, I know you would want me to tell you if I saw one of your crew stealing."

"You damn right, now come on let's go eat." She replied as they approach the counter.

"Hello ladies, welcome to Six Feet Under; how many people are in your party?"

"It's just the two of us hun," Lissa replied.

"Ok follow me and I'll get you seated, did you guys want a table or booth?"

"We'll take a booth, is that cool with you Melissa?"

"Yes, of course."

The hostess leads the ladies through the crowded sea of

tables and over against the wall to a dimly lit booth.

"Here you are and your server will be with you shortly."

"Thank you!" Both ladies reply.

"So how was your honeymoon?"

"Damn, jump right to it, why don't you?"

"Girl you went to Dubai, I want to hear all about it."

"It was relaxing, we really enjoyed ourselves except for a minor hiccup, but I took care of that."

"Oh shit, what happened, I seen that look before."

"Well you have to promise not to repeat what I am about to tell you."

"Melissa my lips are sealed."

"You say that now, but as soon as you get to gossiping over in your shop all kinds of news just seems to get broadcasted."

"I have never said anything about you and your business, I swear."

"You better not Britt or I'm going to beat that ass."

"Well excuse me Miss Thang, you don't have to get violent, now spill the beans."

"Ok so I slept with my Boss a few times before Rich and I got married, we were on a few business trips and after some drinks one thing led to another and so on and so on."

"Hold on, I want details!"

"Another time for that, anyway this fool has been texting me non-stop since my wedding day."

"Wow, are you serious?"

"Is he married?"

"Yes, 15 years!"

"Damn, does she know about you?"

"I doubt it, he says he plans on leaving her but that's neither here nor there at this point."

"Well do you have feelings for the nigga, Melissa?"

"Not really, I was just doing it because it was convenient and shit he's my Boss, I enjoyed the perks!"

"Ha-ha!" Both the ladies enjoy a laugh together at the comment.

"Does Rich know?"

"Hell naw girl, that boy will kill me and Bill too!"

"So what's the plan then are you going to find another job, what?"

"Hello ladies my name is Katie and I will be your server, can I start you guys off with some drinks?"

"Sure, can I have a Mimosa?" Melissa replies.

"And I'll take a Cosmo," Britt replies.

"Alright I'll be back shortly."

"You know what Brittany I really like my job and I make good money, but that may have to change. Bill is getting out of hand. This fool even showed up on my honeymoon."

"Hold up, you mean that crazy came to Dubai?"

"Yes!"

"Bitch what kind of pussy you got!"

"I'm serious! Rich almost caught me talking to him in the bar at the hotel too, but I said some slick shit."

"Child you need to come to brunch with me and the girls next week. They can help you get out of this mess."

"What girls?"

"My strip club partners!"

"How are those chicks going to help me and my situation?"

"Look don't underestimate the shake dancers, they deal with different relationships every-day. So believe me when I tell you that your drama is petty compared to the lies they have to tell to keep that cash flowing."

"Alright I guess, just let me know when."

"Indeed."

"Ok ladies here are your drinks, are you ready to order?"

———————

While his wife entertained her new found friend, Rich finally manages to get up from bed and make it over to the shop.

The tension in the air was so thick in the lobby that you could have sliced it with a knife. Joyce continues business as usual while Rich sits in the office watching her every move on camera with disgust.

The shop was too busy to approach Joyce about the matter now, but he wasn't about to take his eyes off of her. Rock hung around the inside more than usual to also keep an eye on things, the last thing he wanted was for Rich to go off on Joyce while there were customers on the lot.

Only a few hours were left before sundown and Rich's

temper grew hotter within every minute. Neither Kevin nor Melissa was there to cool him down, but he could hear their voices in the back of his mind as he pondered the obvious and upcoming conversation. He gazes over to the cameras monitoring the lot to see how many cars remain to get an idea of the time frame. Rich decides he wasn't going to wait until sundown, instead he chooses to approach once the last customer leaves; so he texted Rock to come to the office.

"Bro I need you in the office, ASAP!'

"Alright, I'm on the way Rich!"

Rock hurries to the office passing several patrons as they exit the building. Only one older gentleman remained in the lobby. He sat there quietly reading today's edition of the Atlanta Journal Constitution then suddenly a quick breeze flaps the pages as Rock zooms by.

"Where are you going, Rock?"

"In the office Joyce, where does it look like I'm going?"

"You don't have to get smart negro."

He nonchalantly ignores Joyce as he enters Rich's office.

"Yo what's wrong man? Is everything ok?"

"Yeah, I need you to do me a favor."

"Sure what is it?"

"Go man the counter while I have a sit down with Joyce."

"Damn, you're about to have that conversation now?"

"Yes I am; why did you ask? Is something wrong?"

"Nah, I got you."

"Good, now tell Joyce to bring her ass in here."

"No problem, I'm on it."

Rock leaves the office then slowly walks over towards Joyce's desk. He stands beside her and waits quietly for her to get off the phone. Joyce places the headset on the receiver then looks up at New York.

"Why are you standing over me like that boy!? What's your problem?"

"I'm not the one with the problem baby, Rich wants to see you in his office now."

"For what?"

"Go find out, I got this."

Joyce begins to feel an unsettling feeling in her chest as her hands seem to start shaking. She had an idea what the meeting was about, but not really. The thief replayed every unlawful transaction in her mind's eye to see if she could have left any evidence.

It didn't really hit her until she spots the camera above Rich's door that overlooks her desk and the lobby, the same one that was there for the past two years. Joyce wanted to turn around and run for it, but she convinced herself that the meeting couldn't possibly be about her stealing; besides Rich loved her like family and he trusted her just the same.

"Hey what's up Rich, did you want to see me?"

"Yeah, have a seat. I need to show you something."

"Sure, what is it?"

Rich picks his iPad up off the desk, puts in his security code then presses play on the video.

"Watch this and tell me what's going on there."

Her palms begin to sweat as her knees shake at an enormous rate. She was caught red handed; tears fill the wells of her big brown eyes as she watches herself steal from the man that treated her like family for years and years. With a frog in her throat, Joyce opens her mouth to explain.

"Rich I am so sorry but but-

"But what Joyce, do you understand how much this shit hurts? I can't believe that you are stealing from me after all we've been through!"

"I needed the money Rich, I was going to replace it, I promise."

"Joyce if you needed money that bad, why the fuck didn't you just ask me?"

"I don't know, I'm sorry, please don't fire me. I need my job."

"What, I can't tell!"

"I'm sorry Rich, I'm sorry; what can I do to make it up? I'm sorry!"

Joyce puts the iPad on the desk then gets up and walks over to Rich and sits on his lap.

"Joyce, what are you doing?"

"I'll do anything you want Rich, anything!"

She leans in to kiss her Boss on the lips, but he resists.

"Don't get carried away now, I'm a married man and this isn't you, so stop acting like a slut."

"Rich please let me make it up to you, I'll make love to you every day, give you head, cook, clean your house, whatever you want! Please!"

"Go sit your ass down and tell me why you needed to steal my money."

She stands to her feet and leans against the desk while facing Rich. Tear drops fall rapidly from her cheeks to the floor as she starts to explain.

"It's Sonny," she replies calmly.

"What about Sonny, is he ok?"

"No he isn't. Sonny has cancer and my mom can't afford the

treatments alone, so I was trying to help out and I was doing ok for a while but but-

"Damn, I'm sorry to hear that, why didn't you come to me?"

"I was going to but you were never at the shop when I needed the money."

"Pick up the phone and call Joyce."

"You were getting all set for your big wedding and honeymoon and I didn't want to ruin it."

Rich stands to his feet, places both hands on his desk to the right of her then looks into her weeping brown eyes.

140

"Dammit Joyce, just go home and see about your brother. We'll talk tomorrow about some family insurance plans. I'll call my agent and have her call you."

"Oh my God, thank you Rich! Thank you!"

"Yeah, don't mention it; tell Sonny to hang in there and tell mom hello for me."

"Ok I sure will, and thank you again!"

Now happier than she could ever imagine, Joyce runs out of the office passing Rock and the last paying patron of the evening as they exchange currency at the counter.

Bitter Sweet

Several days had passed since the Blackmon's returned from their Dubai honeymoon. All of the events that unfolded during that time left much to discuss as they both sit up in bed conversing about work.

"So did you fire Joyce?"

"Nah, I didn't."

"Why the hell not?"

"Calm down baby, it wasn't that serious. She needed the money to help pay for her brother's cancer treatment."

"I wouldn't care if she needed it to pay her momma's light bill. She still stole it!"

"Well she's my employee and I'll handle it how I want."

"Alright big money grip. Is she at least paying you back?"

"Yeah, we're working out something. How did your date go with Britt, what's she talking about?"

"Just girl talk, we didn't discuss anything in particular. We're going to meet again in a week or so."

"Yep, that's your new buddy."

"Can't I have some friends Rich?"

"Hey do you baby, just don't get caught up. You know you're a square."

"What do you mean by that?"

"Never mind, I didn't mean anything by it."

"Whatever! I'm going to make some coffee, do you want a cup?"

"Yeah, bring me one too."

Melissa makes her way into the kitchen just as her phone starts to buzz from an incoming text message. Rich picks it up off the night stand. The name associated with the number read William Kennedy. Rich peeps up at the room door then looks back down at the phone and starts to read the text.

"Hey my love I enjoyed dinner at Houston's the other night. Here are the pics we took."

"What the fuck!" He shouted.

"What's wrong hun?"

"Nothing baby!"

He looks back at the phone. Three images followed the message. Rich couldn't believe his eyes, there was his wife and her boss kissing each other and taking selfies. Right this moment that weird gut feeling that bothered him since that uneasy night in Dubai had come to fruition. Rich, now angry as hell begins talking to himself.

"I can't believe this ho, she has the nerve to act like she's innocent. I bet this bitch has been screwing him ever since she's been working there."

Rich jumps off the bed then paces back and forth in his room while stroking his beard with his right hand. Four blood veins appear across his forehead as his upper lip snarl over to the right. All he could envision were those days when he ran the streets equipped with two nines, a crew and a bad attitude.

He flips up his mattress then grabs the loaded 357 that he kept there for safety then heads to the kitchen.

"You stinking ass ho! Get out of my house before I kill you! Right now dammit!"

Rich points the pistol at Melissa and demands she leaves.

"Richard what's wrong? Why are you pointing that gun at me??"

"Shut up and get out! I knew you were cheating on me, I knew it."

"Cheating! I'm not cheating on you hun!"

"Stop lying Lissa! William just text you and sent pictures of you two kissing at Houston's. Get out now woman!"

"Hold on hun, let me explain!"

Pow! Pow! He pops two shots into the kitchen wall. Melissa runs for the door.

"Rich please don't do this!"

"If I have to shoot this gun again Melissa it ain't gone be pretty! Leave my house!"

"Can I get my shoes?"

Pow! Pow! He shoots two more bullets and this time they pierce the wall by the door causing her to finally leave the condo. Rich picks his phone up off the kitchen counter and calls Rock.

"Hey boss, what's up man?"

"Yo I need you to get the twins together and I want y'all to go ruff this punk up for me."

"Hold on, is everything alright?"

"Nah, I just caught Melissa cheating on me with her boss. He's this tall skinny white guy."

"Damn, that's fucked up! We can put that chump to sleep son. Just say the word."

"Nah, but you can make him wish he was dead though."

"Consider it done, send me his picture."

"I'm sending it now, he works in the Clermont building on the 55th floor."

"Cool, I'll round up the twins and we'll let you know when it's done. Are you sure you don't want him sleep?"

"Yeah and make that fool bleed good too."

"Got it son!"

Beneath the anger he was heartbroken; Rich really thought that she was the one.

Perhaps this was karma paying him back after all the women he dogged out over the years. Now the condo was quiet again and he found himself all alone just that quick. This wasn't over and he knew it, but Rich would have the last laugh.

Melissa, dressed only in her pajamas, walks down to the street to catch a cab. She waits and waits until finally one comes by and stops for her.

"Hello Ma'am, where to?"

"Hey can you take me to the Clermont building, I left my

purse at the office. I can pay you when we get there."

"Sure no problem, I can do that, but its 10 O'clock at night, the building may be closed"

"Great, I'll pay you double because we have to come back here to get my car and I have a key to the building."

"Ok Ma'am!"

Lissa gets in the back seat and leans her forehead against the door window with her eyes closed. Flashes of the last 40 minutes replay over and over in her head as they approach the Clermont building. She knew this was most likely the end of her infant marriage, but the question she wrestled with was if it was guilt that she was feeling or relief?

The 60-story tall transparent office building was dark except for a few offices on the 35th and 59th floor. Melissa exits the cab and makes her way up to the building to speak with the guard at the front desk.

"Hey Mrs. Blackmon why are you here so late?"

"Hi Michael, I forgot my purse and all of my things are in it, can I use the security key for a minute?"

"Sure here you are, just drop it off on your way out."

"Thanks Mike, you're a life saver!"

"Anything for you, Mrs. Blackmon!"

The unusual silence in the huge building felt kind of creepy to Lissa, after all, she was used to the everyday hustle and bustle of normal business hours. The long ride up to the 55th floor amidst the noise from the AC units and elevator cables made her cringe as she passed every floor. Ding! It was odd to see the front desk with no Ingrid there to greet her, but she forged on to her

155

office. There in her top drawer she retrieves her back up cell, car keys, $500 in cash and emergency credit cards that she kept for moments like this. Melissa turned on her cell, went to settings then synced her accounts, emails and contacts with her other phone.

"There! All set!" She spoke aloud.

Hurriedly she walks back to the elevator and heads back down to the taxi.

"Here you go Michael, thanks a million!'

"You're welcome!"

Mrs. Blackmon jumps into the cab as she scrolls through her mobile contacts until she finds Brittany's number.

"Ok, take me back to the condo so I can get my car."

"Sure, no problem!"

She taps Britt's number to make a call.

"Hello this is Britt, whose calling?"

"Girl this is Melissa, I'm calling you from my back up cell. I need a drink-- where are you?"

"Oh hey girl, the ladies and I are heading over to

Pappadeaux's on Mansell road! What's up, is everything ok?"

"Child I'll tell you all about it when I get there. Rich and I had a fight; he found some pictures of Bill and me at Houston's."

"Oh damn, they weren't no x-rated photos were they?"

"They might as well have been! I'm sure we're done. That nigga pulled out a gun on me!"

"What! You are bullshitting!"

"I wish I was, look I'll be there in a few, I'm heading over to get my car now."

"Ok babe, see you in a bit and be safe!"

"Yeah, later."

Every bone in her body wants to text Bill to warn him about what just happened. She knew it was late and texting at this hour could cause even more problems, so she decides to wait until morning.

"Ok ma'am, we are here."

"Thank you, how much do I owe you?"

"The total is $75!"

Melissa reaches in her pajama pants then pulls out a $100 bill.

"Here and keep the change!"

"Thank you, Ma'am!"

"You're welcome."

Melissa steps out of the taxi and walks over to her white 2015 BMW 750 while pushing the trunk button on her remote. She reaches inside and unzips her red gym bag then pulls out her blue sweats and grey Air Max. Mrs. Blackmon opens the back driver side door, sits on the edge of her seat and strips down to her bra and panties then slips on the sweats and sneakers before taking the wheel.

She starts her car then heads down I-75 to the GA-400 and decides to call her soon to be ex-husband while in route.

Chance would have it that 104.1 FM was playing *How Deep is Your Love* on the quiet storm just then. Ring-Ring! Ring-Ring! Rich's cell rang several times but no answer. Tears slowly drip from the corners of her eyes as she opens the sun roof in hopes that the night air would dry her face before she got to exit 8 on the GA-400.

Beep-Beep! Cars blew repeatedly at her as she unknowingly ran the red light in route to Pappadeaux's entrance. Melissa, in a daze keeps going until she reaches the parking lot then parks in the first empty space that she sees. She looks in the review mirror and fixes her hair, wipes her face and puts on some lip stick then proceeds to the entrance while texting Brittany.

"Hey, I'm at the front."

"Hey, we're in the booth over by the bar!"

"Ok, coming now!"

"Welcome to Pappadeaux's, how many are in your party?"

"Hi, I'm meeting some friends-they should be over by the bar."

"Sure, it's to your left Ma'am."

"Thanks."

As she approaches she could hear Brittany's voice among others full of joy and laughter.

"Melissa! Hey girl, come on over and have a seat! This is Blu and that's Jay!"

"Hello ladies, I'm Melissa!"

"Hi Melissa," they both replied.

"I'm glad you could make it. Sit down and take a shot, it's been waiting on you."

"Oh really, and what kind of shot is that Britt? It's Patron girl; what else?"

Lissa downs the shot as the ladies egg her on.

"Go Melissa! Go Melissa! Go Melissa! Yaaay!"

"So tell me what happened, Lissa?"

"Britt it caught me totally off guard. Remember I told you about Bill right?"

"Yeah I do."

"Well we went out to dinner the other night to discuss my marriage and the affair that he and I had going on."

Intrigued, Blu and Jay lean in over the table to hear the conversation.

"Did you two call it off?"

"No we didn't."

"I thought that you loved Rich."

"That's just it Britt, I love both of them."

"Bitch you don't need to be married, you're a ho!"

"Excuse me Jay or whatever your name is!"

"Hold on Melissa, before you get all out of whack baby girl, I'm just saying that you like to be a player that's all. The last time I checked there wasn't anything wrong with that. Hell I'm a player, Blu is a player and so is Brittany. We just need to teach you how to play the game sister that's all."

"I think it's too late for that, Rich will never take me back."

"Well that depends on how bad you want him!"

"I don't know Britt…"

"Girl you need another shot! Waiter! Waiter! Bring us another round!"

One drink led to another and another while the ladies all discussed how they played the many men in their lives with Melissa. Reluctantly she took it all in, hoping that there was a silver lining amidst all the hoopla.

———————————

Three days had passed since that hazy night at Pappadeaux's. Melissa, with her new found confidence and outlook on men decides to give her ex a call. Rich flips through the TV channels with his remote, looks down at his phone then taps the ignore button. It rings again, but this time the name on the caller id reads Joyce.

"Hello?"

"Hey Rich, are you busy?"

"Nah, just sitting here watching TV, what's up?"

"I really need someone to talk to, can you come meet me? Please."

"Sure, is everything ok?"

"No it isn't, Sonny passed away yesterday and I haven't been able to sleep," she replies with a crack in her voice.

"Damn I'm sorry to hear that, did you eat anything?"

"No, I've been too stressed."

"Meet me on the roof top over by Legal Seafood's, we can talk there then get you something to eat."

"Ok what time?"

"I can be there in 15 minutes."

"Alright-- thank you so much Rich, I really appreciate you."

"Don't mention it. I'll see you in a little bit."

"Ok."

Cool brisk air from the AC on the dash of his Porsche was a delightful feeling in contrast to the warm red leather seats that cradle his physique. The Atlanta sun baked everything in its wake and Rich's white ride had no favor. As he cruises past the Georgia Aquarium and down to Marietta, Rich makes a right in front of Stat's Sports bar then a quick right into the parking deck in route to the top level.

The power of Rich's souped up engine echoed throughout every level as he sped to the top. Then just as he reaches his destination, there she was leaning against the trunk of her yellow 2015 Chevy Camaro. A devilish grin masks Rich's grill as he admires Joyce's vulnerable beauty.

Her butter toffee toned skin complemented her red platform heels and cherry sun dress. Rich slowly brings his cocaine white Porsche to a stop then puts it in reverse and backs in to the empty space beside her. He could feel his nature rise at the sight of Joyce's naked body under her dress; her nipples reciprocated the feeling as the warm breeze wrapped the thin cloth around her hour glass physique. Rich watched her mouth move, but didn't hear any words coming out through her white teeth and red lined lips.

"Hello Rich! I said hey Rich!"

"Oh I'm sorry Joyce, you look beautiful!" He replies as he steps out of his car.

"Thank you. I'm glad you came, I really need someone to talk to right now."

"It's the least I could do. I have no idea what you are going through. I'm sorry that you lost your brother."

Joyce walks closer to Rich as he opens his arms to give her a hug. Her soft breasts against his chest only made matters worse. Deep inside he needed someone to hold just as bad as she did. The two fragile souls found themselves in between the Camaro and Porsche as their tongues begin to dance with one another's... then she asks.

"Rich, what about Melissa?"

"Fuck that slut, we're getting a divorce."

"But-"

Rich ignores her and continues on as she follows suit. Joyce reaches down and unzips his pants just as he lifts her up onto the hood of the warm Porsche. Neither one of them seem to care about the patrons walking down below, or about the ones across the street atop of the other buildings looking on. To both of them this day felt like the beginning to the rest of their lives.

———————————

"So tell me again Rock, why are we going to this building?"

"I already told you twin, Boss needs us to rough up this chump."

"Man I'm on probation, I ain't trying to get in no damn trouble bruh."

"Man would you stop acting like a punk and let's just do this shit. We're almost here so chill."

"Rock, what does this dude look like?"

"Here, look at the text from Rich, that's the fool right there."

"Aw man this is a white boy, what the hell he do to Boss?"

"That fool has been sleeping with Melissa!"

"You serious?"

"Yep. Now when we pull into this parking garage put on the damn mask."

"How do you know what level he's going to be on Rock?"

"He's one of those executives so he's got a parking space on the upper deck with his name on it."

"What's his name?"

"William Kennedy."

"Alright let's do this so I can get home, my girl is cooking fried chicken tonight!"

"Ha-ha! Twin your brother is a greedy nigga, I see why he's bigger than you."

"Rock, that boy been like that our whole life."

"I bet. Ok, put on the mask, we're almost to the location."

Rock and the twins drive up to the executive parking level of the Clermont building slowly and make sure that they read every name plate. The twins removed the plates from the rented U-Haul truck earlier so that they wouldn't get made by any cameras.

"Yo Rock, that's it right there it says… Bill Kennedy!"

"Ok what time is it, he leaves the office at 6:30 Rich said."

"Man, its 6:29!"

"Cool, y'all get it out and hide behind his car, when he comes out, jump that fool and throw him in the back of the U-Haul. I'll be back there with some rope and tape."

"Rock are you serious about this man, I ain't tryna get locked up behind some pussy that ain't even mines."

"Twin, just shut up and go get ready, hurry up!"

The twins pull down their black ski masks then proceed to hide behind Bill's black Mercedes Benz as Rock parks the truck a few steps away. Then just like clock-work right at 6:30 PM Mr. Kennedy enters the garage and makes his way to his car.

Bill reaches in his pocket for the keys as he approaches the driver side door. Just then a loud voice startles him.

"Hold it right there Bill!"

"Oh shit, here take my wallet and here's my keys… just don't kill me!"

"Damn your bitch ass sure gave it up quick!" Bap!

Twin clocks William in the head with a tire iron as his brother grabs both of the target's arms and he forces him into the U-haul.

"Get your white ass up. It's a whole lot more where that came from cowboy."

"Look I'll give you anything you want! Please don't kill me!"

Twin slides up the back door of the truck to find Rock waiting there with a wooden baseball bat, dressed in a black ski mask and wearing black gloves.

"No, no, no, please I don't want to die!" He shouts as the twins toss him in the U-haul.

"You should have thought about that before you went sticking your little dick into married pussy, Bill!"

"Wait, wait what?"

Rock revs back the wooden slugger over his right shoulder then follows through with a ferocious swing towards William's knee caps as the twins pin him down to the floor by holding down his hands and legs.

Wap! "Oh my God please stop!"

Wap! Wap! Rock swung again and again bruising Bill's knees with every bone crushing blow.

"Holy shit, please stop, please."

Wap! Wap! "Fuck you Mr. Kennedy and I'll stop when

you stop sleeping around with married women."

Wap! "No more, I can't take anymore!"

"Twins do y'all hear a little punk screaming for mercy??"

"Hit his ass again and make this fool scream louder, I believe he think this is a game."

Rock gets down on one knee then leans in over William.

"Rich says that you can have Melissa's whoring ass."

Bill looks up at Rock with a crushed soul, bloody knees and hurting heart.

"That son of a bitch, he's going to pay for this."

Wap! Rock swings again and cracks William in the mouth.

"Bill don't you even think about retaliating. You're lucky he told us not to kill your ass tonight! Twin, kick this piece of shit off the truck and let's go."

The brothers roll William off the bed of the U-Haul and onto the parking garage floor as Rock made his way back to the driver's seat. Mr. Kennedy was barely breathing, watching the truck speed down to the lower level as he took the cell from his pocket to call Lissa.

Affair

Ring-Ring! She looks at her phone and really doesn't want to answer. Melissa was still trying to figure out how to tell William that Rich saw his text messages the other night. Ring-Ring! Going against her gut feeling she decides to answer. Ring-Ring!

"Yes Bill, what is it?"

"He knows!" With a grunt in his voice, he replied.

"Why do you sound like that? What's wrong? Who knows what?"

"Your husband, he tried to kill me."

"You sound crazy, where are you?"

"I'm in the parking garage sitting in my car, I think my nose is broken and, and, and my arm."

"Oh my God, stay right there. I'm on the way down!"

Lissa runs out of her office and down the hall shouting as she passes Ingrid.

"Call 911, Mr. Kennedy has been hurt!"

"What?"

"Ingrid, call the damn cops!"

"Yes Ma'am, where are you going?"

"To the parking garage!"

Melissa runs down two flights of stairs and into the parking deck until she makes it to William's car. He's sitting there bleeding with his left foot on the cement, door ajar while leaning back in his seat with a bloody nose.

"Bill, Bill, are you alright?"

"No your crazy husband sent some guys to kill me!"

"Are you sure that it was Rich, what guys?"

He slams his left hand on the steering wheel in frustration and yells out.

"God damn right I'm sure, they told me that he sent them!"

"This is crazy, just stay calm, the police are on the way!"

"No don't call the police!"

"Why not?"

"They're going to come back and finish me off if you do! I can't tell them who did it, I can't!"

"Look at you Bill, there's blood everywhere, your nose is broken and probably that arm too! We have to do something!"

"Melissa we can't, your husband is crazy and those guys were serious!"

"What did they look like Bill?"

"I don't know... they wore black ski masks and gloves. I'll just tell the cops that they tried to steal my car and I fought them off."

"This is insane, I'm calling him now!"

"Who are you calling?"

"Shut up William!"

Full of anger she pulls out her cell and proceeds to call Rich. His phone rings several times, but no answer, so she calls again and again until finally...

"What the fuck do you want Melissa?"

"Are you crazy? You didn't have to do this!"

"Nah, that's where you're wrong, you took me to play with. Now I'm gone show your ass how crazy I am."

Click!

"Oh no this nigga didn't just hang up on me!"

"Melissa come take me to Grady, my nose is killing me!"

"Hold on Bill!"

Lissa attempts to call her husband again. Ring-Ring! Ring-Ring! Ring-Ring!

"Rich are you going to get that?"

"Don't pay that phone any mind Joyce, that's just Melissa trying to call me about some bullshit."

"Are you sure because I can leave, I don't want to get in the middle of you guys' break up."

"She's the one that got caught cheating, not me, so fuck her!"

"Well since you put it that way, I guess she won't be needing all of those nice clothes and red bottom shoes in that closet?"

"Joyce it's all yours honey, take anything you want!"

"Nah, I don't want her stuff, I want my own."

"We can do that too baby, I tell you what!"

"What?"

"Bring me all of her clothes out of the closet, including them red bottoms. Let's make room for your new wardrobe."

"What are we going to do with them?"

"I got an idea… just go get them."

Rich walks into the kitchen and retrieves a bottle of lighter fluid from the cabinet then picks his matches up off the counter. He opens the patio door then lifts the lid of the grill.

"Bring them out here Joyce; it's time to have some fun!"

"Boy you are crazy! She's going to be so mad at you."

"Does it look like I give a damn? Now give me something to burn!"

"Ok, if you say so!"

Joyce proceeds to bring every Versace, Prada, Vera Wang, Gucci and Louis suit bag to the patio. She stacked the cream Louboutin boxes one atop of another and brought them out as well.

"Damn, this is a lot of money right here Rich, you are insane!"

"She doesn't give a damn about me, so the hell with it!"

Rich picks up two of the cream boxes and sits them on the grill then soaks the boxes in lighter fluid.

"Joyce can you bring me my cigar off the counter baby and pour two glasses of wine for us. This is a celebration of new beginnings."

"Sure, be right back!"

Richard flicks a match and drops it on the fluid soaked box then admires the bright yellow, blue and orange flames as they dance through the expensive fabric.

Knock-Knock!

"Hey babe, someone is at the door!"

"See who it is Joyce!"

She walks over and takes a look through the peep hole.

"It's that guy Kevin!"

"Let him in!"

"Ok!"

"Hey Kevin, Rich is out on the balcony."

Kev enters the condo a little confused; this wasn't the scene that he was expecting. The last time they spoke this girl was a thief and Rich and Melissa was fresh off their honeymoon.

"Kev I'm out back bro, grab a beer out the fridge then come join me!"

"Alright, I'm coming. Excuse my manners Joyce, how are you doing?"

"I'm ok! I can bring your beer out."

"Cool, thanks! Rich what the hell are you burning up man?"

"Well, right now this is about $6000 worth of shoes and all of that shit right there is next!"

"Man what is all of this and where's Melissa?"

"Bro, I thought I told you!"

"Told me what?"

"Man, that ho has been cheating on me with her boss, that fool sent her some text messages a few days ago. She was in the kitchen when the text came through so I picked up the phone and those two were on there all hugged up and kissing. I kicked her out that same day!"

"Well, you know that I always had a bad feeling about her bro."

"Yeah, yeah I know."

"So what's up with sticky fingers?"

"Man, that's another story, hand me that Versace bag!"

Melissa waited patiently by William's bedside for the doctor to come back with the x-rays. She watched him sleep like a baby while induced with heavy pain killers and notices that his phone is vibrating then picks it up and sees that it's Bill's wife.

"Excuse me, Mrs. Kennedy the x-rays came back positive for the broken nose as well as the right arm."

"Thanks, but I'm not Mrs. Kennedy, I'm his co-worker."

"Oh, my apologies Ma'am, do you know how to contact Mrs. Kennedy?"

"I'm sure that her number is in his phone."

"Well Miss-

"It's Blackmon!"

"Miss Blackmon, can you call her?"

"I'd rather not, maybe one of the nurses can."

"Sure thing, I'll just ask one of them. Are you sure that you don't need anything?"

"No I don't, but I was wondering, how long will it be before his arm and nose heal?"

"At least 6 to 8 weeks. You can just page the nurse if you need anything; I'm going to get someone to contact his wife."

"Yeah, ok."

Bill slowly lifts his head as the doctor leaves the room.

"What's wrong with being Mrs. Kennedy? I told you I was leaving my wife for you, so get used to it Melissa."

"William Kennedy, neither you nor I are in a situation that will allow us to get married. Just take it easy over there; the doc said that your nose and arm are broken."

"Yeah, I figured as much."

"Are you sure that Rich did this?"

"One hundred percent sure Melissa and he made sure those goons delivered the message!"

"Well I tried to call him, but he didn't answer."

"What were you going to say? Do you think I should call the police anyway?"

"Nah, that's not necessary."

"That's easy for you to say! You're not the one all broken up."

"Bill I'm not sure about all of this, I mean look at us. Did you even tell your wife that we're having an affair?"

"No not yet, but your husband damn sure knows!"

"William I can't believe you!" Another female voice replies.

"Oh-um… hey Mrs. Kennedy!"

"Is this true Bill, are you sleeping with this bitch!"

"Hold on, I ain't no bitch!"

"Baby, I was going to tell you!"

"When William? Ingrid told me that you were here and I rushed right over to find you two discussing your affair. Oh my God, you're going to get yours Mister! You'll be hearing from my lawyers, just wait! I can't believe this!"

"Baby wait a minute... this doesn't have to get ugly."

Lissa leans back against the room door, her arms folded while watching the couple argue. She knew this day would eventually come, but had no idea that karma would reveal itself so soon. Mrs. Kennedy storms out of the room as if Melissa wasn't even standing in the door way.

"Now what? This is a big mess!"

"Don't worry about it, baby, as soon as we leave here we can go over to my penthouse."

"What penthouse Bill?"

"You know the one off Pharr Road."

"No, I didn't know anything about it William."

"Well, it's where I go when I need some time alone."

"You're just full of surprises aren't you? I know there better not be another woman over there because I ain't that little woman that just stormed out of here. I'll break your other damn arm."

"Melissa-

"Don't Melissa me!"

"Is everything ok in here, Mr. Kennedy?"

"Yeah, of course, Doc!"

"Ok good, the nurse is coming in to prep your arm for the cast and I have this splint for your nose."

"I'm going to get some coffee Bill, I'll be right back."

He looks at Melissa and gives a nod as the Doctor helps him up to the sitting position.

Separation

A loud car horn sounds off repeatedly causing Rock to turn around with the shop keys in his hand as he was just about to open the door for him and Joyce to start the day. The loud horn from a brand new all black BMW X5 sounded off again and again to get their attention.

"Who the hell is that, they need to hold up for a few minutes. The crew isn't even here yet."

"Go tell them it will be a few then Rock, I'll start the generators for you."

"Thanks Joyce and don't forget to unlock the back door for the crew."

"Ok Rock, I got it."

"Cool let me go see who this is."

As he got closer to the X5 the driver side window began to roll down slowly. Rock slowed up his pace then approached with caution just as a male voice spoke out.

"So did y'all rough that fool up last night?"

"Damn Rich, we didn't know who you were son. I thought you were a customer."

"My bad bro I just picked this up for Joyce."

"Damn nigga, should I steal from you so you can buy me a car too!"

"Man don't start that bullshit, I'm fucking her so she gotta be rolling clean brother!"

"Yeah, whatever but we worked that punk over real good last night. I know he has to have some broken bones."

"Good, I'm gone take care of y'all too. I appreciate it!"

"Hey, I enjoyed it myself; it's been a while since I had to crack someone's skull."

"I figured you would. How did the twins handle it?"

"Those two thugs enjoyed it more than I did."

"Bet that. Did you leave him a message?"

"Yeah, he knows you were behind it."

Rich steps out of the X5, gives Rock a pound then heads inside.

"Yo, keep an eye on this for me; I'm going to get Joyce."

"Sure boss!"

The steady sound of generators and the air conditioning unit brought an unusual calm to the atmosphere inside the lobby. Joyce's high heels made a clacking sound as she walked across the ceramic tile on the way to her desk.

"Hey you!"

"Oh hey Rich, what are you doing here so early? You were still asleep when I left."

"Turn the radio on then come outside for a minute I have something to show you."

"Ok, is everything alright?"

"Yeah, come on!"

Joyce feels nervous because of Rich's abruptness, but she cautiously makes her way over to the door where he stood waiting.

"Do me a favor and park that X5 over by your car."

"What? Why can't one of the guys do it?"

"Woman I'm still your boss, don't get it twisted."

"Ok, ok, let me have the keys."

She walks over to the black BMW X5 admiring its beauty and the way it sat on the black 20" mag rims. Joyce opens the door and before she sits down she spots a card on the seat with her name on it. Joyce knew the card was from Rich, but wasn't sure if she should open it. Besides it hasn't even been three weeks yet and he bought her a car? Going against her nerves Joyce opens the card and it read:

Thanks for being there when I was in a rough spot. You don't know how much that meant to me. Please accept this gift as a token of my appreciation.

Rich approaches the X5 just as she finished reading.

"So do you like it?"

"Rich you didn't have to!"

"I wanted to; so it's yours. Now start it up and take it for a drive around Buckhead."

"But-

"Don't worry about the phones we'll cover them until you get back. Remember, I did say only go around the block, right?"

"Yes Rich!"

"Oh ok just making sure!"

Joyce jumps in, starts the ride and speeds off the lot.

"Damn son, that girl is going to get a ticket today if she's going to be driving like that."

"Rock chill, she'll be alright."

"I'm just saying!"

"Man how about getting the crew over here to handle these

cars that's pulling on the lot. Let me worry about Joyce."

Rock looks over at Rich with a curious grin then heads to the employee locker room to round up the crew. This was a side of Rich that he'd never seen and he didn't like it.

Several weeks pass and the leaves begin to turn from green to orange and then brown. One hundred degree days had transformed into 65 and 70 degrees. The Atlanta Hawks became spectators as the Georgia Dome came to life with the Dirty Birds and the Yellow Jackets, Bulldogs and Panthers compete in their NCAA conferences.

Melissa and Bill find themselves sitting on the deck of their new mansion during Saturday College Game Day watching the Bulldogs take on the Gamecocks on their large flat screen.

"Bill I have a question?"

"Yeah what is it?"

"When are you going to sign those divorce papers?"

"Melissa I told you that we still have some things to iron out. She wants too much money and I'm not agreeing to her terms until she comes to her senses."

"Well, I sure hope that she comes to her senses soon because I'm not going to be living with a married man. My divorce will be final soon and I expect the same from you. If you can't make that happen, I'm moving into my own place."

"Baby I'm legally separated so it's not like your messing around with a married man anymore."

"Fuck you Bill! Get it done, you were committing adultery too."

"Ok, ok just calm down I will."

A ten foot tall wooden privacy fence secured the large

backyard and its fresh cut grass. Several imported California Palm trees align the fence and over shadow the heated man-made waterfall pool and Jacuzzi that sits in the center of the yard.

Lissa, now frustrated stands to her feet, removes her shirt then heads towards the oasis.

"What are you doing?"

"I'm sick of your shit William, I'm taking a dip and no I don't want you to join me."

"But you look so sexy with just your thong on!"

"Stay there Bill!"

"Do you want your phone? I think it's ringing because Brittany's name is flashing."

Lissa turns around and heads back towards William to get her cell.

"Here you go, it just stopped."

"Thanks!"

She looks at the missed call log to see who called. The first name on the list read Brittany so she returns the call.

"Hello bitch, where have *you* been? We haven't seen you since you and the white boy got serious."

"Hey Britt and cut it out. I've just been busy."

"Hey baby mama!"

"Who was that?"

"Girl that's Blu, she said what's up."

"Oh tell her I said 'Hi'."

"Um Hmm, so what's new? We need to catch up."

"Well, I will officially be divorced in a few weeks. Rich just need to sign the papers."

"Congratulations I guess! Are you happy?"

"Not really, but can you guys help me move my things after the divorce is final?"

"I don't know about Blu, but I can help you chick."

"Thanks Britt, I appreciate it."

"Wait a minute, what am I getting out of it? I'm gone need a drink, Louis bag, Car or something?"

"Brittany you're a nut! We'll figure out something."

"Ok cool! I'll call you later; I need to finish Blu's hair."

"Bye Britt."

"You think you're slick don't you Brittany?"

"What are you talking about Blu?"

"You just want to be alone with Melissa's fine ass. I heard her ask us to help her move."

"Nosey! Stay out of my business."

"It was my business too until you excused me out of the equation."

"Girl, be quiet before I shave all of your damn hair off."

"Ha-ha! Ha-ha! Don't play Britt!"

Divorce

Rich gathers himself just before exiting the car while thinking it seemed like only yesterday when he married the woman of his dreams. He puts on his Burberry aviator shades and walks towards his attorney's office. A slight fall breeze wraps his khaki slacks around his ankles as he buttoned the blue blazer he was wearing over his yellow Polo shirt that complemented the blue Polo loafers.

Hundreds of patrons stroll to and from the Dekalb County Courthouse as he approached the adjoining plaza making his move to the law firm entrance.

"Hello welcome to Kerry Jones and Associates, how may I help you?"

"Yes, I'm here to see Miss Jones."

"Sure, do you have an appointment?"

"Yes, can you tell her that Richard Blackmon is here."

"Sure-- I'll phone her now."

"Thanks."

"Hello Miss Jones, there's a Mr. Blackmon here to see you."

"Thanks, can you tell him to have a seat; I'll be out in a minute."

"Will do."

"Sir, she'll be out in a minute, you may have a seat if you like."

"Ok, no problem."

"Can I get you a drink of water or some coffee?"

"No, I'm fine but thanks."

"Oh, you're welcome."

"Mr. Blackmon!" A female voice sounded out.

"Hello Kerry!"

Rich couldn't help but to smile from ear to ear as he laid eyes on his stunning attorney. Kerry had the beauty with the brains and power to match. Her chocolate colored skin appeared to be smooth as milk under the peach blouse and blue dress pants she wore. The white of her big brown eyes glowed even brighter when in unison with her perfect pearly smile.

Ms. Jones wore peach colored Jimmy Choo shoes and smelled of Illicit Parfum of the same brand. Her silky black hair bounced off her shoulders as she approached Richard with an extended hand.

"Hi darling, are you ready to be a single man again?"

"You don't know how ready I am!"

"Awesome, come with me, I have the papers from Melissa's lawyer. It took some negotiating, but I'm sure you'll be happy with the terms."

"Good, let's get this over with."

"Alright follow me, Sir. Oh sweetheart, can you block out the next hour for me?"

"Got it covered Ms. Jones."

"Thanks you're such a doll!"

"Richard, its right this way, follow me."

They took a few steps down the hall then entered the second door on the right which led into a conference room that held a large stainless steel table with a walnut finished top that was surrounded by several black leather chairs. A pitcher of water and three glasses sat in the center just in front of Rich's case files.

"Ok have a seat and let me tell you what's going on Mr. Blackmon."

"Alright shoot!"

"Well, at first your ex was trying to get half of your businesses, but since you did the smart thing by placing them all in Nevada Corporations I managed to side track that fiasco. She doesn't have the time or money to take it there with me!"

"Wow! She's the one that cheated and she feels that I owe her something. You have to be kidding me!"

"I'm afraid not Rich. If you want my opinion, I think she still wants to be married to you."

"Yeah whatever, what else?"

"She says that you caused physical damage to Mr. Kennedy. Is there any truth to that?"

"I don't know what you're talking about."

"Well if so, you need to tell me so that we can be prepared for criminal charges."

"Trust me there's not going to be any charges."

"Are you sure about that?"

"Positive!"

"Good! Well I got them to agree on an amicable split. You keep what's yours and she keeps what's hers."

"Sounds good to me. It was going to be some problems if that bitch had any other ideas."

"Oh she had plenty, but let's just say I earned my pay."

"Well, thank you. Where do I sign?"

Kerry slides the files over to Rich and hands him a pen.

"Right here and then again on pages 12 and 22."

"Ok cool."

Richard signs, closes the folder and stands to his feet.

"Thanks a lot Ms. Jones, I really appreciate this."

"You're welcome Mr. Blackmon I was only doing what you paid me to do."

Kerry and Rich find themselves standing face to face looking into one another's eyes as he reaches out to shake her hand.

"Well thank you!"

"Oh Rich there's one more thing."

"What's that?"

"Don't you ever spend any of this money? I have to say that I was pleasantly surprised when I reviewed the books from the shop. Is there really that much money in washing cars?"

"See that's just it. It's more than washing cars."

"Please explain!"

"See our customers come to us because they know that we will keep their rides clean inside and out. Think of it like you think of your beautician. Some folks look at their rides the same way."

"I guess, but it still eludes me. Anyway, I was thinking about investing in some property like that shopping mall you have down at Myrtle Beach. How can I get my hands on some opportunities like that?"

"My good friend is in the business; that's who put me on. I'll pass your number on to him."

"Awesome, that would be great. Oh and there's just one more thing Rich."

"Yeah what is it?"

"We should do dinner sometimes."

"Really, I would have thought you were involved, gorgeous as you are."

"Don't let the looks fool you darling, most guys are scared of a woman like me."

"Well, I'm not and we sure can, just call me sometime. I have to be going."

"Alright you can count on it, take care."

Rich makes his way down the hall then exits the firm and reaches for his cell to call Kev.

"Hello!"

"Kev, what's up bro, are you busy?"

"Nah man, just watching some game high lights. What's going on?"

"I need to pick up some things from Joyce's place. Can you help a brother out, we need your hands and your truck."

"Of course bro, what time?"

"Now!"

"Damn negro!"

"Kev her place is two blocks from your house on Pharr. Her address is 285 unit 678."

"Ok, I'm on the way."

"Cool, see you in a few! I'm like 10 minutes out."

"What, you're not even there?"

"I'm on my way, bruh."

"This is gone cost you some Gladys and Ron's!"

"I got you Kev, I got you!"

"Ok see you over there."

As Rich weaves through the Buckhead traffic he couldn't help but to think back on all of the signs he had missed. He turns down the car radio and opens the sun roof to feel the fall breeze and listens to the sound of the city. Right then he made a vow to himself to never be played like that ever again. It was time for the rebirth of Daddy Rich. He looks in the rear view mirror and smiles at the thought. Beep-Beep!

"Hey you motherfucker! Get the hell out of the way, the damn light's green!"

Rich snaps out of his daze and proceeds to make a left onto Pharr Road and into the garage of Joyce's apartment where Kev sat waiting. Rich comes to a stop in front of him and rolls down his window.

"Man how did I beat you here and how much stuff are we moving?"

"Bro I was stuck in traffic."

"Rich it wasn't any traffic, don't even try it."

"Kev chill, you're getting some food out of this deal so that means no complaining."

"I'm just saying!"

"Bruh, let me park the whip and we don't have that much. It's clothes mostly and she wants her flat screen."

"Yeah ok and hurry your ass up."

_____

Just a few blocks away Melissa and Britt enter her old condo to collect her things.

"So tell me why do you still have the key?"

"He never asked for it back. I'm surprised he didn't change the locks!"

"Me too Lissa, you would've thought."

"Girl it doesn't matter, just help me get my designer shit out my closet that's all I really want."

"Alrighty then, I know you gone let me get one of them designer suites."

"Nah Britt you need to let me hold something, I know you caking over there at your shop."

"Who, not me!?-- I do alright."

"Yeah, umm hmm. Come on the room is over here and why do you have that big ass purse with you?"

"Oh I stopped by Starship right before I met you. I bought a new toy."

"What kinda toy? Never mind don't answer that."

"Melissa it smells like a bitch been in this room girl."

"Britt so what if it does, we're officially divorced, that man can do what he wants. What the fuck??"

"What's wrong Lissa?"

"The damn closet is empty, where are my things?"

"Stop playing, where could they be?"

"I don't know Britt; help me look for them, check all the closets, drawers, under the bed, everywhere!"

"Ok, ok, Melissa calm down, I'll check the other room while you look in here."

After three painful trips up and down the staircase, Rich and Kev had finally packed all of Joyce's things into his truck.

"Bruh you didn't tell me the elevator was broken."

"Kev I found out the same time that you did."

"Well at least we're all done; let's stop by the gas station on the way out. I need a Gatorade or something."

"Man your ass ain't tired; stop tripping."

"You're right, I'm not but I am a little thirsty."

"I'm just fooling with you Kev. Oh I almost forgot…"

"Forgot what?"

"My lawyer wants to meet you, she was asking about my property down at the beach and I mentioned your name."

"You think she's ready to get involved with Real Estate?"

"I don't know the answer to that, but I can tell you she's one of those fine ass successful chocolate sisters."

"Is she fine like Gabrielle?"

"Finer!"

"Damn alright, set that up."

"I already got the number for you."

"Rich don't get me in no trouble."

"Bruh what trouble, your ass is single!"

"Yeah funny, how did the divorce proceeding's go?"

"It's all done, no crumbs, no strings."

"Cool, now you can get on with Joyce. I still can't believe you two are seeing each other after she's been stealing from your ass."

"Kev don't even go there, you showed up at the reception with Sybil."

"See that was just a friendly outing, two friends coming to support another friend."

"You don't have to explain to me, I'm glad you're out there doing the playboy thing. Come on let's get these boxes over to the crib so we can go get some chicken and waffles."

"Now you're talking my language. Rich you're alright I don't care what them ho's say about you."

"Ha-ha! I'll meet you over there in a few."

 Brittany removed the covers off the guest bed, stormed through the closet and even looked under the bed, but there was no sign of Lissa's things.

 "Girl I done looked all over this place and I didn't find one shoe, sock, dress, bra, nothing. I'm going out on the balcony to hit this blunt."

"Ok Britt, I need to check the master bathroom closet."

"Yeah alright and come hit this blunt when you can't find shit!"

The ladies conversation goes up a few decibels as they converse between the bedroom and balcony.

"Girl you're a thug, when I first met your ass you was all quiet!"

"I was just being like that around Kevin's mean ass. Bitch I think I found your stuff!"

"Britt, oh my God! Where is it?"

"Um, come out here on the balcony!"

Melissa runs out of the master bathroom, through the bedroom, the living room then out to the balcony and stops in her tracks.

"Oh no this bastard didn't burn my shit!"

"Melissa I think you better hit this blunt."

Lissa, in awe at the charred remains of her designer suits and shoes atop of the open grill falls to her knees with tears in her eyes. Brunt fabric covers the balcony floor as the fall breeze blows ashes of expensive clothing around the two ladies humbled bodies as Britt held Melissa in her arms.

"Come on baby, let's go inside-don't cry it was only clothes. It all can be replaced."

"It's more than that Britt. He hates me that much that he burned my things. I would never do this to him."

"Lissa, I mean you were fucking your boss."

"Britt shut up!"

"I'm sorry, come on let's go inside."

———————————

The time was 7 O' Clock pm in the ATL as the fellas parked in front of Rich's building to unload Joyce's things.

"Rich your elevator does work, right?"

"Yeah man, just grab the boxes and let's get this stuff upstairs. I'm starving."

"That makes two of us, I'm right behind you."

Rich opens the gate of Kev's SUV to retrieve a few boxes then waits for Kev to grab some.

"Bro stack those two on top of these, I can take a few more."

"Are you sure Rich? We don't need to be dropping nothing."

"Yeah, put them on here."

"Alright, here you go."

"Thanks!"

"No problem, I'll just grab the flat screen. I don't think we should leave it down here."

"Kev seriously, is that all you're going to take up?"

"Bruh, this thing is fragile!"

"Man, come on and let's go. I can't believe you."

Kev slides the flat screen under his right arm and walks ahead of Rich then opens the door to the building. They bypass the security guard at the front desk and proceed to the elevators.

"Good evening Mr. Blackmon!"

"Hey man, how are you doing?"

"I'm good Sir! Do you guys need any help?"

"Nah we got it, just keep an eye on our cars, we have a few more boxes in them."

"Sure thing, Mr. Blackmon!"

As the elevator doors open Rich makes his way inside then leans the boxes up against the walls to keep them steady.

"Man you're struggling over there, ain't you brother."

"Don't even try it, mister, I got the TV."

"Did you want me to leave it down stairs? I really don't think you should be moving her in anyway. You just got divorced negro."

"Joyce is not moving in, she still has her place and you don't have room to talk."

"Rich, that Sybil thing was nothing, besides I'm a single man now anyway."

"I am too, the divorce is final, Daddy Rich is back!"

"Ha-ha! Ok Daddy Rich moving a new chic in the same day that you finalized your divorce."

"Look bruh, she's my main girl. I'll be getting me a team together watch."

Ding!

"I hear you Rich; this is your floor right?"

"Yep, come on let's go. Do me a favor and grab that key from under the matt."

Kev squats down with the flat screen under his right arm then lifts up the right front corner of the matt with his left hand.

"There's no key here Rich."

"What, it should be. I have one on my key chain, but it's in my pocket and I can't get to it."

Kev stands up and turns the door knob to see if it was open.

"It's open Rich!"

"That's crazy, I swore I locked it. Come on I must have left it unlocked by mistake."

The fellas cautiously enter the condo being certain to look around for any intruders.

"Oh my God, oh my God!"

"Rich did you hear that?"

"Yeah it's coming from my room."

"Oh my God, oh my God!"

Rich sits the boxes on the floor just as Kev drops the flat screen on the couch and they both slowly make their way towards the room.

"Oh my God, Brittany how long is that thing! Ughhhhh!"

"It's my 10-inch strap on bitch! I call him the black cobra! This is my new toy, how does it feel?"

Melissa, constantly moaning with every deep stroke as she grabs two fists full of comforter with her back arched and ass up in the air lets Brittany stroke her from behind.

"Ummm, it feels great! Do it harder, harder!"

Simultaneously Rich and Kev stop in the door way of his room, shocked at what they were seeing.

"Melissa you slut, get the fuck out of my house!"

"Oh shit Rich I'm sorry- nooo, nooo Britt don't stop!"

"Brittany! What in the hell?"

"Kevin!"

Thank you for reading the second installment of **Pulsations of a Heartbeat**: *Unholy Matrimony*. I hope you enjoyed it and be sure to check out installment three in the **Pulsations of a Heartbeat** drama and suspense series by fellow Author, *Lorenzo 'el Gee' Gladden*. Please don't hesitate to leave a review on my Amazon or Barnes & Noble comment forums. I would love to hear from you! If you want to contact me directly, you may do so via Printhousebooks.com

ANTWAN BANK$

Other titles available from this
Bestselling Author:

Amazon Bestselling Trilogy

The MADE Crime Thriller Trilogy is about Andy Cooper, a military vet turned hustler, turned Gangster, turned Crime Boss. His marriage is on the rocks; fresh out of the military, AC finds himself broke and lost with a wife and three kids to feed. Trapped in Sin City and working any job he can get from day to day to make ends meet. Hating the state of mind he's in right now is a really fucked up way to be! Gone are the days when Uncle Sam paid for housing, day care and groceries. Now, he's all on his own again with no idea of where life is going to take him. One thing for sure, Andy "AC" Cooper no longer wanted to wear that Army uniform another day. Coop loved every minute of it and would not trade it for the world, but the next chapter of his life was about to start. It just so happened that he landed in Las

Vegas, one of the hardest cities to make it in, it is truly the land of the hustler. What the outsiders don't know is that beneath the bright neon lights, the delicious buffets and luxurious casinos, lays a whole different world that would eventually suck him in.

The word Adoration can be defined as fervent and devoted love or simply put: to worship. During our time on Earth we will all experience this powerful thing called Love. This novel will take you on a journey seen through the eyes of four couples and their relationships. For Love we endure amazing things and some of us will go to the limit to keep it.

ANTWAN BANK$

Love can fill your heart with joy or leave it filled with hate. Adoration explores love at several levels, some of them good, some bad. In Book One of this Series, hearts will break, tears will fall, blood will shed and bells will chime; all in the name of love.

F.I.T.H. is a Drama about a High School freshman and a bully. The situation becomes very intense when the bully doesn't let up. Although the victim tries his best to have tolerance and handle him accordingly, no matter what he tries, nothing seems to work. After several run-ins and close calls, the victim is forced to become the Bully's favorite mark, influenced by a perpetual presence of fear, his life as he knew it-- changed.

These collections of spirits were some of my favorites to mix for the thousands of customers that I served as a bartender back in my 20's. During 1995 - 1996, I worked as a bartender in several Las Vegas Clubs and had a damn good time doing it! I've included a few recipes I picked up from fellow bartenders, some from customers and most I've learned from Bartending School.

Mixology is an art and if mastered, one can make a really good living serving spirits and conversing with the people you serve at your bar. If you're a bartender looking for some new drinks or you're just someone interested in mixing up some new drinks in your kitchen, this book of spirits is for you. Welcome to the Party Life and remember to drink responsibly.

Miss Jones, Book 1 of Series.

The Cover Girl series is about, an Atlanta Eye Candy photographer named Malakhi Jones. Pronounced (Mal uh Ky). This short story and many others to come will take you inside a day in the life of a hot photographer and his daily encounters with several of the industries sexiest Magazine Models and Video Vixens.

While these events are Fiction, anyone in the industry knows what goes on at the shoot, stays at the shoot! Malakhi is at the top of his game and he's connected with every

Men's Magazine Publisher, Casting Director, Hip Hop Artist and Talent Manager in the industry. Getting a session with him is like winning the lottery when it comes to being an eye candy Model, in the ATL. Any Model knows, that once the session starts and that camera flashes, all rules will be broken to obtain that success. If not, then keep dreaming!

In book 2 of The Cover Girl Series: Lola Love, *Malakhi ventures on a location shoot with the Sexy Chocolate Video Vixen, Lola Love. Her enticing aura almost proves to be too much for the A List Photographer, but in true Malakhi fashion, he prevails. The two meet up, downtown on Peachtree street Atlanta at one of the Cities five star hotels.*

Together, they will create magic for the camera and hot lustful memories in their Jacuzzi Suite. They say a picture is worth a thousand words, but only the photographer and the model know what exactly goes on between those poses.

In book 3 of the Erotic Cover Girl Series: Madam Grace, *Malakhi encounters the lovely mixed beauty Madam Grace. While handling business as usual he soon finds out that this beauty has a kinky side. The photographer however is always up to the challenge and Grace proves to be that and then some.*

From the backdrop of the ATL, the hottest city in the South comes a compelling love story about several friends and their adventures in College at the A.U and their professional careers while in the city of Atlanta. Experience Love, Drama, infidelity and historic memories as you indulge yourself in this Romantic tale of fiction. Set in 2001-2002,

you're sure to reminisce back when Jay-Z, Nelly, Luda, Missy, 112, Lil Jon, Alicia Keys and more were in heavy rotation on your favorite radio station. When T.I's album, I'm Serious, had the city crazy, the clubs closed late and Ying Yang had those ATL Shake stages rocking and dollars raining.

Everlasting Romance: An American Love Story explores the essence of friendships, life, love and how those bonds molded several individuals into a close knit family while in the hot city of Atlanta. Donnie, Quentin, Chantel, Cynthia and their friends found themselves sharing love at every level, Brotherly, Sisterly and most of all intimately! But-- at what cost?

In the City of Atlanta, the Gentlemen's Club Industry reign Supreme. Alongside the fledgling music industry that contributes platinum hits every other month, together they both pull in Billions of dollars each year. You would actually have to live here or frequent the ATL to see the marriage these two have committed to each other.

The biggest misconception is for

someone to assume that it's all illegal. What many don't know, is that the city of Atlanta benefits off of every Stripper, Bouncer, Waitress, Dj and Bartender that works in the Gentlemen's Club Industry. The truth of the matter is, for any girl wanting to strip here in the ATL clubs, such as Onyx, Majic, Strokers, Pin Ups, Shooters, Follies, Blue Fame, Blaze, Oasis, Cheetah, Pleasers, Diamonds, Babes to name a few (And trust me there many more!), you must first have a permit from the County that club is in before you can even think about dancing on any stage in this city.

Yep that's right! These permits can only be obtained from the County Sheriff Department where they perform a thorough background check for Felonies and any open Warrants.

Unholy Matrimony

If you have a conflicting felony you will not get a permit! If you have a warrant, you will not be leaving through the front door, but going to the back in handcuffs instead. Permits range from $250-$475 per year depending on which club you are getting a permit for (That's every-year!). How do I know, you ask? Well, let's just say when I first got to the A, I took a Doorman position at one of the most notorious clubs in Atlanta where I met thousands of dancers who led me to write this story. The club shall remain anonymous because they fired my butt for hustling too hard; Hell, I was just trying to show them how to get paper. After all, I did just close a club back in South Khak that I ran for 12 years. Anyway that's another story.

Regardless of what you may have seen

or heard, the competition in these clubs is fierce and that makes for some slow nights when it comes to the cash flow for some girls. So some of them, more times than not, take it to the next level and do what they like to call private parties. For you squares out there, that means Escorting or Tricking if you want to keep it street.

I found myself in an interesting position while working at this ATL Gentlemen's club. The dancers confided in me and asked me to be their driver to some of these so-called private parties. The stories from those nights and from other private discussions we had while riding in my car were unreal! My true passion and God given talent is as a writer, so I had to ask these girls if I could tell some of their stories, while keeping them anonymous of course. I was

273

happy as a kid in a candy store when they agreed. So here it is several accounts of the ATL night life through the eyes of many dancers that I rolled into one character, whom I named Tahiry. Laced with Cocaine, Molly, Weed, Lean and Z-Bars, this life is in no way full of glitz and glamour; true crime rides along at every turn. From the streets of ATL this is our story, cold Hearted and Street Official. R.I.P to the dancers we lost to the Strip Hustle. We got love for you.

Millions travel to the City of Angel's every year in search of that one shot at stardom. But most fail and find themselves caught in the underbelly with the homeless, the drug addicts, prostitutes, thieves and murderers. Candy and Joe unfortunately are no different than most and end up living in a different hotel every other nigh,; doing whatever needs to be done just to survive.

Gate Key: Turning your High School Education Into Millions attacks the glue that holds the very fabric of the higher learning institutions together. It gives hope to teens that find themselves in despair. It creates opportunity for those in lower class society who seem to be destined for a life of poverty and unemployment. It turns that one way street to becoming a criminal into an 8-lane highway of self-preservation.*

276

Gate Key will not only spark the flame to ignite the inner fire that we call a dream. It reveals over 30 lucrative professions that can be started while in high school or immediately after which will place our youth on a road to success without the need for a college education.

The awful truth is that only 4 out of every 7 teenagers will go on to attend college after graduating high school and for many reasons some will not complete this journey. Everyone wants the American dream for their kids; they want them to get a degree, find a great job, get married and have children, buy a house with a white picket fence then live happily ever after. Here's a shocker! The American dream will be just that for many of our youth, a dream! Too often teens can't afford college, have no interest in going, did not prepare for it, have kids early or are undecided, any one of which causes them not to attend college and to head straight into the sub-par job market. Minimum wage can barely pay utility bills let alone take care of a family; this, more times than not, places our kids in the lowest class of society (in reference to a three-tier society of Lower Class, Middle Class or the Upper Class).

This book gives our youth a choice as to what class they want to end up in, how much income they want to earn and how to begin that journey while still in high school without getting any student loans or attending any college. It will put our youth on track to become prosperous entrepreneurs and professionals by making them aware of career choices that they probably didn't even know existed for them as teens.

Gate Key doesn't only make our youth aware of these opportunities, but will show when, where and how to start one of these featured career paths while still a teen. This book is designed to open doors for those that cannot or will not be attending college after high school for some reason or another. Even now you have the power in you to be whoever you want to be! My purpose is to open your eyes to some of the many options that the world has to offer. After all, it was said best by our forefathers in **The Declaration of Independence***:*

"We hold these truths to be self-evident, that all men are created equal, that they are endowed by their Creator with certain inalienable Rights, that among these are Life, Liberty and the pursuit of Happiness."

Growing up as an African-American, Hispanic or even a poor Caucasian in America is a challenge. The system is built to keep you in the lower class and it has its reasons. Billions of tax dollars are shelled out every year on food stamps, welfare, housing and many other

Government   assistance
programs.

 Even if the beneficiaries of the
above   wanted   to   become
productive citizens in their own
neighborhoods and make it on
their own, they would be hard
pressed. The local education
system as well as the local
economy just simply cannot or
will not support its people, so
other measures need to be put
in place! Some will find the
fortitude to get into college
and/or leave their destitute
neighborhoods   to   become
productive citizens, employees,
business owners, etc. But that
dream is few and far between.

This environment almost always leads to the same impoverished cycle or for many, a life of crime. With no role models, local businesses or community programs around or father figures in many of the homes, the streets usually find a way to take over.

These circumstances are more common than we would like to admit. Many people will turn to the drug trade and some will become thieves, prostitutes, pimps, killers and drug addicts. The harsh reality of your family starving without lights or water will make any sane person do what they need to in order to survive. Compounded with the stress of everyday poverty stricken life, hardcore criminals will emerge with a burning desire to succeed. Whether they take the legitimate route or illegal is the question.

In the culmination of it all, I can assure you that no matter what the decision, someone will be profiting from these inequalities and in that majority will be the private prisons of America. A collective of legal Corporations whose soul survival is to put warm bodies in cold cells to meet a Government contracted quota. Because of this need, Government has no incentive to help these low income communities but to watch them falter instead; it's actually cheaper for them to pay Private Prisons than to invest in these communities-- this giving way to an abundant prison population that serves as the modern day slave trade.

ANTWAN BANK$

PRINTHOUSE BOOKS.

Read it, Enjoy it, Tell a friend.

**VIP INK Publishing Group,
Incorporated.**

Atlanta, GA.

www.PrintHouseBooks.com

Unholy Matrimony